CALCULATED EXTORTION

A Calculated Series Prequel Novella

K.T. Lee

Vertical Line Publishing

K.T. Lee
www.ktleeauthor.com

Publisher's Note: This work of fiction is a product of the writer's overactive imagination. It is not intended to be a factual representation of events, people, locales, businesses, government agencies, or cybersecurity. Names are used fictitiously and any resemblance to actual people, living or dead, is completely coincidental.

Calculated Extortion/ K.T. Lee -- 1st ed.
ISBN 978-1-947870-05-5

Book cover design by The Book Design House
www.thebookdesignhouse.com

THE CALCULATED SERIES

For my family

ONE

Martín Vásquez ran a frantic hand along his nightstand and fumbled his buzzing phone onto the floor. He found the infernal device and squinted his eyes against the harshness of the glowing screen. Those who knew him well did not make it a habit to contact him in the middle of the night, and the message was almost certain to be urgent. Before he could read the lengthy text in its entirety, his stomach dropped. Their hacker had found a way in. Again. He rubbed a hand down his face and reached for his laptop. While he waited for the login screen to appear, Martín reread the message and looked over at his sleeping wife. It was a wonder Camila hadn't awoken from the noise of him stirring or from the force of the tension radiating from his entire person.

When his computer made an ironically cheerful sound, Martín entered his password. A few keystrokes later, it was clear the hacker had made good on his threat. How their attacker had access to his personal cell phone number was anyone's guess. However, it was probably easily obtained by the same person currently holding their computer systems hostage.

Despite the futility of the gesture, he pounded his finger against the enter key on his keyboard with a quiet desperation. It had been over ten years since Martín had a literal gun placed against his head. However, the sinking realization that he had no choice but to do as he was told and hope that he could survive to fight the next battle was exactly the same. Lives would be affected if he didn't pay. Families would go without food and medical care while the insurance company sorted through the wreckage of who was responsible to determine if the charity's policy would cover it. His people were under attack and God only knew what someone like this was capable of if they didn't get what they wanted. At 11:30 p.m., he entered his banking information and hoped that the worst was over.

TWO

Scarlett Callahan had very nearly succeeded in taking a break from her work as an FBI profiler over the weekend. While research showed that yoga and meditation were good for the psyche, she preferred to unplug by redirecting her nervous energy to something more tangible—repurposing antique furniture. Which she did very well…until she checked her email. Scarlett couldn't resist peeking into the one from the complaint department. While working in the complaint department was almost universally dreaded and where new FBI agents were sent to pay their dues, those emails always held the most promise for a bizarre case—her favorite. All manner of crazy non-cases flowed in through complaints but this case had all the hallmarks of a real criminal. By Sunday evening, she had a meeting set up with two special agents and was already formulating a game plan.

On Monday morning, Scarlett arrived at the office early to study the details of her new case before she brought in the agents who would be helping with the fieldwork. Scarlett had recently transferred to the Chicago FBI field office from the National Center for the Analysis of Violent Crime in Quantico, Virginia, and still had plenty of proving herself to do. While the FBI kept a concentration of behavioral analysts, known colloquially as profilers, at the NCAVC, the Chicago field office had enough work to keep a dedicated, on-site profiler busy. When the position in her hometown opened up, she jumped at the chance to come back to the eclectic, busy city she'd never stopped considering her home. She had fewer years of experience than some, but her Ph.D. in psychology and track record of success had enabled her transfer to a position with a higher pay grade and (slightly) bigger office.

Scarlett settled into her desk chair and began to study the meager pile of information they'd collected on the case over the weekend. The ransomware attack at World Partners for Peace was a new twist on an old favorite. While cybercrime had unfortunately become quite common, the extortion of thousands of dollars from a respected charity was unusual, to say the least. She shook her head as she read the summary of who would be impacted by the cyberattack. Fortunately for her, one of her closest friends was an FBI special agent who, like her, specialized in the unusual. She and her partner would be arriving shortly.

The sound of footsteps approaching her office brought Scarlett out from behind her desk and into the small sitting area she'd squeezed into her large-for-the-FBI office. Scarlett had designed her small space to be a quiet haven from the buzz of a demanding workplace. While it was personally nice to have a cozy office, it was a professional necessity. She intended to do everything she could to make sure those who visited it had a clear head without distractions. Hers was a business of mind games, and winning them required attention to the smallest detail. Thus, it had been worth the effort to haul two compact couches through the painstaking security procedures at the front door. Fortunately for her, the antique furniture she preferred was smaller than modern furniture and the reupholstered seats served their purpose of being both comfortable and welcoming. Scarlett laid out two sets of crisp, clean documents on the small coffee table in front of the couches just in time for Alexis and Parker's arrival.

"Hey Scarlett!" Alexis Thompson walked into her office carrying two coffee mugs. Alexis wore a pair of neatly-tailored gray pants and a blue dress shirt, and her hair was pulled back in a bobbing ponytail. As usual, her eyes were bright with purpose. She held out one of the mugs to her friend and Scarlett smiled when she saw the tea bag floating at the top. Alexis gestured to her own cup. "I would have brought you coffee but…"

"Yeah, I'm not that desperate. Blech. I mean, thank you." Scarlett wrapped her hands around the warm mug and lifted it to her old friend. While many of her colleagues willingly drank the dark substance that came out of the communal pot the Bureau swore was coffee, Scarlett had her limits. There was a café in the building for those that weren't brave enough to consume the free stuff, and Scarlett was a regular. However, she'd arrived today before the small café even opened, and tea was the safer choice.

"Morning, Dr. Callahan." Special Agent Parker Mitchell entered the room and nodded at Scarlett before closing the door behind him. Parker picked up the papers she'd laid out and settled on the couch to study them. Scarlett didn't know Parker well yet but Alexis spoke well of him. While Scarlett was still forming her opinion of Parker, the approval of the whip-smart, no-nonsense Alexis spoke well of her more quiet, serious colleague. Parker projected a calm and competent demeanor, and most importantly, he was low maintenance. He said what he meant and meant what he said. That wasn't the sort of personality trait that Scarlett took for granted. He looked up from his reading. "Must be big to have such an early meeting."

Scarlett took a sip of tea. "It isn't big…yet. Just unusual."

Parker raised an eyebrow. "It's never good when you've weirded out the psychologist." Alexis rolled up the sheets of paper Scarlett had placed on the table and used them to whack Parker in the shoulder, who remained unmoved. "What? She's seen it all and she's friends with you. She's got to have a high threshold." Alexis raised the paper again and Parker held his hands up in surrender. "So, what's up, Scarlett?"

Scarlett plucked the paper out of Alexis' hand, unfurled the weapon and flattened it on the table. Alexis raised her mug to her face to hide her grin. Scarlett and Alexis had been close since they'd been assigned to the same dorm freshman year. Alexis didn't share

Scarlett's Ph.D. in psychology but her work as an agent for the FBI had further developed her considerable natural talent of reading people. Despite not realizing how much her new job jitters were on display, Scarlett felt her shoulders relax while refereeing Parker and Alexis. Alexis, to her credit, didn't look too smug.

Scarlett cleared her throat and began. "Yesterday, we received a call from the CEO of World Partners for Peace, Martín Vásquez. World Partners is one of the largest donors to sustainable development initiatives and crisis medical care both in the States and abroad. His insurance company required that he let us know that his computer systems were hacked. They were taken completely offline. Martín received an email immediately after the system went down, demanding a ransom to turn it back on. The amount was small and he paid it."

Parker sucked in a breath. "That's a dangerous precedent."

Scarlett nodded. "He panicked. He was worried it would affect the people they support. He just wanted it to be over."

Alexis furrowed her eyebrows at the notes on the table. "Does he know who was responsible?"

"No idea," Scarlett said.

"So what if it was just a test? You have the good faith of a hacker that they won't do it again?" Parker asked.

Scarlett sighed. "I don't think he was given any sort of guarantee. Not that it's worth much coming from someone stealing from you, anyway. In his defense, he probably didn't think he had another option."

"So, what's the plan to stop it from happening another time?" Parker asked.

"It already did. His contact with us only occurred after the hacker had taken over the system a second time. It happened late Saturday night, ten days after the initial attack. This time, a text message was sent to his cell phone. The first message was all business but the second message was a little more personal."

Parker whistled. "Okay, I get it. He tried to keep it under wraps until it happened again. Now they're panicking."

"Exactly," Scarlett said. "And the last time Mr. Vásquez paid the ransom, he received a follow up message." Scarlett looked down at the paper. "'Strike Two. Want to see what else I can do?'"

Alexis scrunched up her nose. "Ew. Someone wants attention."

Scarlett nodded. "And they're getting it. He contacted his software providers immediately after the first attack but they didn't find the hole the hacker used to get in either time. That means they probably left the door open and are planning on coming back."

"What kind of person goes after a charity? And what if our hacker turns violent?" Alexis asked.

Scarlett placed the mug of tea on her desk. "Both good questions. We don't have a lot to work with from the message alone. We should presume our hacker is capable of escalating to an in-person attack. Most hackers don't want to risk coming out from behind the curtain but the tone of the message Mr. Vásquez received last weekend suggests it's personal. Unit Chief Sandhill asked me to take the lead on this case but we don't have much to go on. I need you guys to find out what you can on the ground. There's a person hiding behind all of this code. Take some time to digest the details of the case and we'll meet up again soon."

Alexis picked up the paperwork and rose to leave. "Please tell me you are talking to Jordan about this today."

Scarlett nodded. "My next stop is his desk." Scarlett had only been in the office for a few weeks, but Jordan Sykes' knack for getting into locked computer systems was well-known within the FBI, even outside of his home base of the Chicago office. He'd consulted on one of her investigations in the not-too-distant past and made a break in a case that had most of her best people at Headquarters stumped.

Parker said, "We should get Mikey on this. No one bullshits him and we could use the extra set of eyes."

Scarlett looked up from her paper. "Mike Moretti? Seems to be pretty sharp from his reports. Is he in the office? I haven't met him in person."

Alexis and Parker exchanged a look. Parker said, "Mikey's happiest in the van, where he doesn't have to talk to people."

Scarlett raised an eyebrow. "And this is the agent you want helping us?"

Alexis shrugged. "He's one of the best we've got. Don't worry, his bark is worse than his bite."

A glowing recommendation wrapped in a hedged statement wasn't exactly the sort of reassurance Scarlett was looking for. However, in her experience, like attracted like. Parker and Alexis had the kind of reputation and respect in the Bureau that went well beyond their years of experience. If they trusted him implicitly, she'd at least give him a chance to prove himself. "Okay, bring him up to speed if you think we need him. I better go find Jordan."

Scarlett navigated a series of wide hallways until she came to a nondescript black door at a dead end. She ran her badge over the small black box next to the handle. Upon receiving a green light and shrill chirp, she pulled the door open. The lights were off inside the large open room that housed the cybersecurity team. Not surprisingly, it was mostly empty. While most of the analysts on the cybersecurity team kept later hours than the more traditional agents, Jordan Sykes was one of the few that was consistently present during normal working hours. He sported his usual clothing: ironically out of date sneakers, a zip-up sweatshirt, and jeans. Prior to his second career working for the FBI, Jordan had been trained by the best in Silicon Valley, founded a company, and sold it before age thirty. After the requisite lengthy application process, Jordan proudly referred to the FBI as his retirement job. He sipped from a large, shiny can of energy drink with angry letters scrawled across it and raised it to her in salute.

"Wow, hitting the juice pretty early this morning, Jordan? That can't be good for you."

He grinned and took another swig as she wrinkled her nose. "Good morning to you too, Scarlett. In my defense, it's actually late, not early. I was up all night working on this one."

"You didn't come in last night, did you? I emailed you to let you know we were going to be talking about it this morning. I didn't mean for you to pull an all-nighter. Did you break any laws?"

Jordan cracked his knuckles and grinned. "Says the person sending me emails on a Sunday. And no. But if I did, you'd never know it." When Scarlett put her head in her hands, he chuckled. "I just peeked to see how vulnerable their systems are. It actually looks good. I haven't found a way in from the outside just yet."

"Really?" Scarlett said.

"Yeah. I even threw out a couple of phishing attacks to see how easily I could fool the people who work there. They were beautifully done, but no bites yet. It's still early, but they've got people who actually know what they're doing." Jordan looked away from Scarlett to glare at the lines of code that were nothing but garbled letters and numbers to her.

"You know, you're supposed to consider that good news."

Jordan gave a long-suffering sigh. "Technically, yes. But that means I don't have any more information for you. Whoever broke in is top notch if they went from the outside in. You sure they couldn't find a trail on the inside?"

Scarlett looked at the file again. "The CEO said someone from IT checked the history of every person who logged into the system and they couldn't find a record of anyone using their permissions to shut the system down. We also have the analysts tracing the source of the messages to the CEO but haven't had any luck on that either. It just isn't that hard to buy an untraceable cell phone."

Jordan rubbed his face. "Yeah, this is definitely my department. Do me a favor, though. Get some feet on the street and see if the CEO is hiding anything. Does he owe any money? Would it be to his benefit to fabricate the story?"

"I'll get the team working on it. Also, what about the IT guy who checked the access of everyone who was in the system?"

"Yeah, him too. You never can tell with the computer nerds." Jordan grinned and went back to the task at hand.

"Don't forget to get your paperwork in order if you want to try and jailbreak the system, Jordan," Scarlett said over her shoulder as she left.

"No having fun without your permission. Roger that."

THREE

With her team assembled and fully briefed on the case, Scarlett began the afternoon in a trendy but modest waiting room at World Partners for Peace. The charity had a reputation for doing meaningful work and had a large staff to support their efforts. Their headquarters was substantial for a non-profit—it took up an entire floor in one of the many skyscrapers in downtown Chicago. Despite his busy schedule, Scarlett had arranged a meeting with the CEO with only one quick phone call that morning. Then again, it wasn't every day the CEO of a huge charitable organization was being personally targeted by a hacker.

The CEO's assistant called her name. Scarlett stood, straightened her black suit and pulled her notebook out of her handbag. Scarlett tapped lightly on his open door before entering. Martín Vásquez was middle-aged, with only the slightest paunch, brown eyes and thinning salt and pepper hair. The corners of his mouth were turned down when she entered his office, but he rose from his desk to greet her. His welcome was warm, but his eyes were cautious.

"You must be Dr. Callahan. I'm Martín Vásquez. Thank you for making the time for me." Martín had barely a trace of the Argentinian accent he'd likely had when he immigrated to America some thirty years prior. He'd applied for US citizenship as soon as he was able and received it after a lengthy waiting period, according to his records. Martín placed himself back behind his desk and carefully folded his hands on top of it. While his smile was pleasant, his feet, made visible by the minimalist design of his desk, pointed towards the exit. She could hardly blame him for wanting to bolt, but she was there to determine if his desire to leave was because he wanted to find the hacker or he was afraid the FBI would find out he was guilty of the crime.

"Yes, I'm Scarlett Callahan, FBI. It's very nice to meet you. Of course. We'll do whatever we can to help."

"I think the damage has been done." Martín met her eyes and Scarlett let the question hang in the air. After a few seconds of uncomfortable silence, he began to backpedal. "I mean, the risk gets higher every time they break into the system. Surely they won't try again. Don't you think?"

Scarlett reached into her bag and pulled out a pen to buy time before answering. She was cautious in her habits as she frequently spoke with frightened witnesses and liars. Still unsure of which one she was dealing with, she stuck to her plan. "Let's see, your systems went down twelve days ago until you paid a ransom. It happened again in very much the same fashion two days ago. Given the contents of the text message you received, what makes you think this individual would stop?"

"They have everything they asked for. I don't know why they wouldn't quit while they're ahead." He rubbed one arm as he waited for Scarlett's answer, only stopping to adjust his tie. Digging for her opinion while nervously fidgeting; yeah, she'd let him sweat a little longer. She took a few extra seconds and ran a finger down her page of notes.

"Did you track the payments back to the source?"

Martín rubbed his face before returning both hands to the top of his desk. "No. They requested we use a type of digital currency." Scarlett winced. Their criminal's use of cryptocurrency would give them yet another layer of data to dig through. "The software companies we use for our computer systems are just pointing at each other and my IT expert hasn't been unable to track it any further. So we came to you guys."

She almost called him out on the lie but instead decided to see how far he took it. The original intake report stated that the insurance company would not reimburse them for the attack unless they reported it to the authorities.

Martín looked up at the ceiling and back at her with a red face. He added quietly, "And the insurance company required we contact you. We wanted to try and stop it on our own first. We should be able to stop it. I mean, I've been kidnapped before. Just one of those where they stop you on the side of the road at gunpoint until your family pays. Not like a real kidnapping. What I mean to say, is that I thought we could handle something like this on our own."

Excess storytelling could indicate truthfulness and his nervous behavior could reasonably be attributed to distress. Martín Vásquez certainly had reason to be distressed. Well, shoot. He still might be the good guy after all.

Scarlett turned to a blank page in her notebook. "Catching a hacker is harder than it sounds, and your thief seems to be escalating his or her attacks. That's why we're here. Do you have any reason to suspect someone would target you or your organization?"

Martín pulled a handkerchief out of his pocket and dabbed at his face. "Not really. It seems they could have picked a number of better targets."

Scarlett chose not to point out that since they had successfully extracted money from his organization not once but twice, their culprit had done a pretty effective job of picking a target. Morality wasn't always a factor for the types of people willing to commit these crimes. "Let's pursue that line of reasoning. If the charity is not a good target, they might have had opportunity. Do your systems have any known vulnerabilities?"

"We've never had an incident before this, and we're as careful as we know how to be. We regularly receive financial information about our donors and our recipients. The nature of the information we possess can be quite sensitive and we thought we were well-protected.

Under the circumstances, I thought it was wise to pay the ransom after I logged in and verified the systems were locked down. Shortly after I paid, I received a security key that let us get everything back online."

"And did they gain access to your financial information?"

"There's no sign of a breach. I recommended we bring some outside experts to verify that, just in case we're missing something. My IT director is still looking but I am told it's not always easy to tell. So, we'll have to let you know." Martín's voice cracked and he swallowed hard. "Does this sort of thing happen often?"

"Often enough that the FBI has a cybercrime division, I'm afraid. We're concerned about larger attacks, such as on our infrastructure, but occasionally, companies get hit too. Something like this gets high priority in case it's just one piece of a broader attack strategy or someone testing out their ransomware at a small scale before going global with it."

"Oh. I never considered that."

"We unfortunately see these things too often. It's important to get any trace of the ransomware removed in case your hacker left a way back in. You've done that, right?"

Martín paused too long before answering with a question. "And your team can help us with this?"

Scarlett winced. "I'll have someone from our team reach out to your IT contact. I'd like to recommend that you allow a couple of agents from our Chicago office to come in and discreetly talk to your people. Even with all the advances in technology, there's no substitute for solid, on-the-ground human intelligence. One person with the right access can do a lot of damage without leaving much of a trail. Also, I would limit the spread of information on this as much as possible. I'd rather take our hacker by surprise."

"We've checked our records and are confident our people are not involved in this. Really, we're like one big family."

Scarlett nodded once instead of explaining that there were psychologists whose sole specialty was undoing the damage inflicted by familial dysfunction. "Even families have their own problems. You are now out $30,000 and no closer to finding your culprit. Are you willing to bet on more?"

Martín picked up his phone. "I'll get you what you need. And I won't let my people know the FBI is involved." Before he could dial, Scarlett held up a hand.

"Mr. Vásquez, before I go, you may want to consider a little extra security until we sort this mess out." The phone returned to its place on the hook and Martín folded his arms on his desk.

"That's not necessary."

"Sir, I hate to point this out, but so far, we keep underestimating our criminal." Scarlett generously used the word "we" because while Martín was a little naïve about his people, he'd turned to her for help, described the situation accurately, and was turning out to be a decent person. More likely than not, he had acted irrationally in his haste to do the right thing and took on more responsibility than he should have. It was hardly unusual for someone in such a high leadership position to rush to handle a difficult situation before it spiraled out of control.

Martín set his lips in a line. "I have a few people that provide security in some of the locations in which we operate. I'll make sure they're around the office. It might not just be me that this person is after."

FOUR

"So, did Scarlett say we get to go out and play?" Alexis said from atop Parker's desk. She'd hopped up into her usual spot and Parker leaned back and crossed his arms in response. Alexis was a close friend and great agent, but she was not known for her patience—particularly when she hadn't been allowed in the field for a while.

Parker raised an eyebrow. "You have a problem, my friend."

"Says the pot to the kettle. Wipe that smile off your face, and I'll believe you aren't looking forward to getting out of the office too. I know you're working on our covers. What do I get to be?"

Parker pulled up a screen and gestured for her to look. "We'll go in as a group. Coming in as donors might cause people to ask questions, so I went with something less obvious."

"Good call."

"Acting like we're in IT will raise suspicions."

"Agreed. So what are we?"

"Efficiency consultants."

"Dear God. People will hate us."

Parker grinned. "Most likely. But if people get worried we're going to come in to lay them off, they might actually answer our questions. We'll start tomorrow." Alexis jumped off of his desk and bumped fists with Parker. Alexis was right—the longer he looked at the files, the stronger his own itch to get out of the office became. No amount of remote research could replace a good conversation.

A message popped up on his screen from his longtime friend and partner in the field, Mike Moretti. His last assignment had ended and he was now available to help out if he was needed. Mike preferred to run point in the surveillance van, but Parker's boss and unit chief, Patrick "Sandy" Sandhill, had an uncanny ability to hone in on and leverage his people's talents. Unfortunately for Mike, and fortunately for the Bureau, Mikey's ability to put together seemingly unrelated details on his cases had not gone unnoticed. It was just a matter of time before Sandy stopped letting him do all of his work in the field and made him spend a little more time in the office, teaching the newer agents. After reading the message, Parker adjusted his plan to account for three agents. Now was as good of a time as any to bring him into this.

Mike Moretti pulled a high-end sedan into the loading zone outside of a building several blocks from the FBI field office. The silver Mercedes drove like a dream but wasn't as practical as his usual ride, an FBI-issued surveillance van. However, like the van, the Mercedes had its purpose. Parker and Alexis appeared from around a corner, and he raised a hand to his head in salute.

Alexis dropped into the passenger's seat. "Hey Mikey. Nice to see you again." She wore a light grey suit and her hair was swept back up into some kind of fancy twist that women did. She didn't quite hide her grin as buckled her seat belt.

Mike raised a suspicious eyebrow. "How long has it been since Sandy let you out of the office?"

"Too long, Mikey. In fact, long enough to even make me happy to see you."

Parker clung to a paper cup of coffee with one hand while he settled into the backseat and gave a sleepy nod in Mike's general direction. Silence was golden for Parker before 9 a.m. Generally, Mike would be happy to ask Parker questions just to drive him nuts, but he was still a step behind on this case. He needed the drive time to process the information Parker had emailed him yesterday. Mike wasn't the type to over-sentimentalize a situation that didn't call for it, but it was hard not to feel some sympathy for a respected charity bleeding out money to pay ransoms.

Like his fellow field agents, Mike was dressed for the role he would play today. Mike wore a black suit and a clean shave. He'd even ran some gel through his black hair this morning to make it look like he was the sort of man who cared about his appearance.

While he was vocal about his preference for working behind the scenes, it wasn't because he sucked at undercover work. He could just process more streams of information if he wasn't in the middle of the action. However, since the new profiler had convinced the CEO to let the FBI come talk to his people, the least he could do was help with some old-fashioned intelligence gathering. Sure, cybercrime was one of the newest types of crime they dealt with, but it still sprouted from the same handful of motives that drove their other perpetrators.

Mike turned the car into an open spot in the crowded parking garage, and they rode silently in the elevator to the World Partners for Peace offices. A cheerful administrative assistant directed the three agents to a computer to register their visit. She hummed as she printed off their temporary badges.

A door swung open and three World Partners for Peace employees filed into the lobby, each wearing a different expression, ranging from discomfort to disdain. Each agent split off from the group to the person nearest them and introductions were made. A thin, older woman clutching a notebook approached Mike with a straight back and tight smile. He held out his right hand when Barbara Rosenthal introduced herself. She offered a hand and kept a firm grip as she looked at Mike over her bifocals, once up and then down. Her eyes narrowed when they reached his perfectly polished shoes. Mike stood a little taller under her appraisal. She released his hand and harrumphed out a breath. "And you are Mr. –?"

"Delaney. Mike Delaney. I'm a workforce efficiency consultant and I'm here to learn more about your charity."

"I'll just bet you are."

Parker was right about at least one thing—everyone was too irritated by his presence to doubt his cover story. Barbara looked like the kind, grandmotherly type, and even she was practically growling at him. Hopefully, Parker hadn't overplayed their hand. Mike acted as if he hadn't noticed her obvious annoyance and continued to follow his planned script.

"Would you mind giving me the tour and introducing me to the staff?"

"Not at all. That's what I'm here for," Barbara said flatly and led him through a glass door into a large common area. There was a low hum of activity through the space. Phones rang and friendly voices recited information while other employees had their heads down at their desk, focused on their work, as if tours like theirs were commonplace. Perhaps they were. That was worth knowing.

"How long have you been with the company, Barbara?" Mike asked Barbara's back, as she led him past a row of high cubicle walls.

Without turning around, Barbara answered, "Charity. You mean charity, Mr. Delaney. I've worked here for fifteen years and am the Director of Donor Relations. This is where our volunteers sit." As they rounded a corner, several young people looked up curiously from their workstations. Four volunteers were crammed into a space slightly larger than a standard cubicle. A poster over the entrance to the area read "Intrepid Interns" above a picture of the impossibly tiny Gemini spacecraft. Funny, but the joke was highbrow humor. World Partners wasn't recruiting just anyone.

"Are they volunteers or interns?" Mike gestured to the sign.

"You pick what you'd like to call them, but they're not paid, Mr. Delaney. You'll want to leave them out of your cost analysis," Barbara said. Three of the four acted as if they hadn't heard the comment but one of the young girl's eyes widened. A gentle elbow from one of her fellow volunteers made her turn back to face her computer, and Barbara began to steer him away from the small group.

Mike sighed. He wasn't going to win Barbara over like this. "Do you mind if I meet them? I'm interested in what they do."

"Okay." Barbara came back to join him at the entrance to the crowded workspace and gestured to each intern as she introduced them. "This is Emma. She's sixteen and manages all of our websites. Susanne is working on analyzing our microloan data to find out where people default and how to prevent it. Bryan is helping us understand how often we lose shipments of food and medical supplies and how that impacts the effectiveness of our programs. Kevin is helping the PR team design more effective ways to communicate via social media platforms. We're grateful for their help."

"Wow. Sounds like they keep you guys busy. Thanks for your help." The interns smiled, all blissfully oblivious to Barbara's disdain for him, except Emma, whose concern for Barbara reached the corners of her mouth. Barbara turned on a heel to continue her tour and Mike gave a quick wave to the interns before following her. As they walked down a hallway, Mike asked, "Do you have any trouble recruiting people to come work at a not-for-profit?"

Barbara paused, turned, and smiled the sort of genuine smile that lit up her entire face, the first he'd seen it since they'd met. "Actually, we have the rare gift of being in high demand. Mr. Vásquez has a reputation for hiring talented, motivated employees. Millennials especially. The media and a lot of for-profits can't seem to figure out what motivates Millennials, but it's simply not that difficult. A lot of them just want to make a difference while making a living wage. Mr. Vásquez can offer that. We're changing the world here, and we have a line of talented people who want to help us do it."

As if realizing once more that he was the enemy, Barbara's features stiffened when she held a door open for him. "And now we have the accounting department." Mike entered a quiet room with several people focused on their computers. While the room was as bright as the main area from the large windows, it was much quieter. It didn't escape Mike's notice that the minute he walked in, someone changed what they were doing on a screen. It was too bad the FBI hadn't convinced World Partners to give Jordan access to the financials, or he'd know what they were trying to hide. Instead, he meandered over to the accountant who was now exuding calm.

Mike extended a hand. "Hi, I'm Mike Delaney. I'm an efficiency consultant."

The woman offered a tentative smile and met his hand with a light grip. "Oh. Hi Mike. My name is Jen Duncan. I'm an accountant here."

Mike smiled a warm smile and gestured to her screen. Acting charming didn't come as easily to him as it did for Alexis and Parker, but that didn't mean he couldn't play the game. "Wonderful. It's very nice to meet you, Jen. Could you tell me a little bit about your job?"

Barbara had drifted off to answer a question, and Jen twisted a pencil in her fingers. "Sure. I analyze charitable opportunities and make recommendations about where we should allocate our funds. I'm focused on individuals who have faced extraordinarily difficult challenges who are a good fit with our mission."

"What types of challenges?"

"Any number of things, really. We could be helping people who have experienced natural disasters, like famine or hurricanes, or those who received a devastating medical diagnosis and the bills that come with it."

"Oh? So you direct the donations?"

Jen gave a wry laugh. "No, I think you have me confused with Martín Vásquez. I just provide information and a financial analysis." There was a bitter undertone in her voice he didn't quite understand. "I'm sorry, Mike, but is the charity losing money or in some kind of trouble?"

Mike laughed an easy laugh. "Just the opposite, Jen. The board of directors just wanted us to go around, talk to people, and see if there were any opportunities for us to help the charity be more efficient. Greater efficiency will allow us to help even more people."

"Oh. I see." Her smile was genuine now and she sunk into her chair as if the weight of the world had just come off of her shoulders. Maybe their covers were too overkill for them to get to the truth. He'd have to tone it down or win Barbara over to get anything useful from his visit. Since the second one wasn't working, toning it down was probably the best option.

"Thanks for your work, Jen." The nervous accountant shook his hand and he found Barbara, who directed him out into the hallway. She'd barely touched his shoulder, but her demeanor brooked no argument.

Barbara said quietly, "It's not easy, you know."

"Pardon?"

Barbara crossed her arms. "It's not easy. No matter what the accountants say, it's not just numbers. There are people behind the numbers. Faces of people we have to turn away because we're trying to make our dollar stretch the farthest we can. We can't ever help everyone we want to. There's only so much money to go around, which means we end up having more heartache here than you might think. Even in accounting."

"I understand. Really, I'm not here to lay anyone off. I'm just here to help." Barbara put her hands on her hips and Mike raised three fingers in the air. "Scout's honor." Barbara chuckled and he took the advantage while he had it. "One last question—is there anyone new here?"

Barbara thought for a moment. "No one I can think of, outside of the interns. And we're lucky to have them. They're either super high achievers or kids who have big stuff on their plates who decided to give back anyway. Emma is a cancer survivor, for example. She went through a year and a half of chemo and radiation at great cost to her family and they don't have much to begin with. She'd barely been in remission three months when she showed up at the front desk asking how she could volunteer because the organization provided her with a small amount of support during her treatment. I can't imagine her medical bills are even paid off and still, she's giving her time. Freely. No questions asked. Now, Mr. Efficiency Expert, what do you say to that?"

"It sounds like you are doing some incredible work, Barbara. Personally and professionally, I thank you for it." Mike held out a hand and after a second of deliberation, she grabbed it firmly and nodded once. Despite all of her efforts to fight it, he'd managed to win her over. While he didn't get much solid information, he'd found a reluctant ally whose motivations aligned with his own. It was a small win, but he'd take it. Barbara led him back to the lobby where Parker and Alexis waited with neutral expressions.

Mike led his team back to the car in silence, but as soon as the doors closed, Parker asked, "What'd you get, guys?"

Alexis scrunched up her nose. "Not much. Talked to the PR people. Didn't get anything suspicious outside of one of the PR reps insisting on following me around everywhere I went. His name was Nick Burket. He was friendly enough but asked a lot of questions about what I was doing and why I was there. Too curious for my liking. His buddies seemed to think he's opportunistic and looking for ways to climb the ladder. Seems like he has a lot of personal ambition for a not-for-profit employee. It could be desperation in disguise. How about you?"

Parker said, "I got put into a room with the people in charge of IT systems. Whole lot of people with special access codes and a high level of visibility to the software used at the company. Pete Smythe, the IT director, was the only one I was sure knew about the hack. He didn't say a word about it when I asked about security. He's in his fifties, married, and shook when he talked to me. Not enough to go on, but worth thinking about. As far as I'm concerned, that whole department is suspect. You get anything, Mikey?"

"Some dirty looks from my tour guide, but she could be an asset later if we need her. I get the feeling her sense of right and wrong is pretty black and white. I met the interns—young and ambitious with pretty varied backgrounds. And apparently one is a teenage cancer survivor. Hard to believe anyone would go after these people."

"Anything else?" Alexis asked.

"Yes. A finance person named Jen Duncan. Didn't get anything firm but she was acting...weird."

"Well, she did have to talk to you," Alexis said and Mike did his best to appear annoyed with her in the rearview mirror. Alexis sighed. "But, since it could be something else, I'll write it down."

Parker said, "Good work, team. Let's write up the reports and err on the side of detail until we figure out what matters. Then we'll pass the information along to Scarlett. She's anxious to make some progress and it's time for Mike and Scarlett to meet anyway."

Mike raised an eyebrow. "I've worked remotely with the profilers in DC for years. I'm not sure why we need to be best friends now that she's in the office."

Parker smiled. "Because no matter how much you think you can outsmart him, Sandy isn't going to let you stay in the surveillance van forever. You're good at strategy, dude. You'll be working with the profiler and everyone else in the office at least once a week before you know it."

Mike grumbled and drove towards the inevitable.

FIVE

T he morning after their visit to World Partners for Peace, Mike dutifully reviewed his notes on every detail of the prior day's interactions. It was too much of a hassle to get video surveillance approved, which meant he had to do everything by hand. He grumbled at his paperwork and scribbled another note. Accustomed to working alone, he didn't consider that he might have witnesses to his annoyance.

"Aw, sitting at a desk too hard for you, Moretti?" Mike looked up from his computers to glare at the two fellow agents carving time out of their day to give him shit. While Mike was a Special Agent and the two men were both Supervisory Special Agents, the formality of the hierarchy didn't extend that far.

"Nah, just got the news I have to spend more time with you two. I've requested hazard pay." One of the men flipped him off, and Mike grinned in response. He fired off his report to Parker and put his head back into the evidence. Halfway through the latest report from the IT team, he got tired of reading. The profiler had noted that she was working with their best IT guy to find the source of the hack. He pushed away from his desk and went to find Jordan. Their best IT guy couldn't be anyone else, and he'd rather hear the latest from the source directly.

Jordan cracked his knuckles without moving his eyes from his monitor, covered with indecipherable code, as Mike approached. He remained frozen until Mike clapped him on the back. "Hey, Jordan. Good work on the charity case so far."

"Thanks, man. Got a lot more to do." Jordan shook his head, as if struggling to break his focus from the task in front of him.

"I've got some questions about our hacker."

Jordan swiveled around in his chair to face Mike. "You and me both. Heard you were on the ground yesterday. What'd you guys figure out?"

"You first. But dumb it down for me. I don't speak software."

"Sure thing. Their IT director, Pete Smythe, believes that ransomware was installed on the hard drive of the CEO's laptop. Once it was connected to the network, his computer was used to lock down the entire network until the CEO paid the ransom. Once he gave me access to their system, I was able to get them a patch for the holes I could find, but he fixed the CEO's computer personally. He seems pretty protective of his systems and is keeping me on a short leash. Bad news is, I can't say that those measures will keep the malicious code from worming its way in again. Oh, and I can't guarantee that the holes I patched were the holes our guy exploited, since even I couldn't even find them all until I was on the inside."

"You're full of good news. So you think someone in the charity is behind it."

"It's possible, but they still aren't willing to let me all the way in without supervision. I can't even prove they're right about how the hack happened. It's clear they targeted the CEO since he had access to the money. Doesn't mean an employee did it. Or if they did, that they even meant to. You can download some of this stuff from a link in an email."

"Did they?"

"Their IT team says no."

"But you aren't buying it. Any success tracking our hacker?"

"One of our analysts dug through the first message sent to the CEO and extracted an IP address out by North Lawndale. It was buried through some fancy footwork but we unwound it pretty far. Big problem is that if they're good enough to do this hack, they're good enough to hide their location."

"We got anything else?"

"Nope."

"Then send me the address."

Scarlett had almost finished clearing her inbox for the day when she saw Mike Moretti's request to follow up on a promising lead that evening. Given that he tended to operate independently, the fact that he was taking the time to formulate a question meant he genuinely wanted her opinion. Answering him swiftly would help build trust between them. His question was a simple one. He had the paperwork in order, so what did she think about tracking an IP address from the first ransomware attack and knocking on doors?

Scarlett tapped her finger on her desk and sighed at the too-short list of information she'd deduced about their perpetrator. *Calculated, patient, intelligent, motive not purely financial(?)*. The only thing Scarlett was truly confident about was that their criminal was going to strike again. A few keystrokes later and he had her approval, if only to eliminate superfluous evidence. It was time to determine who was hiding behind the malicious code and if Mike Moretti wanted to knock on a door to help her find their guy, she'd take it. If she had her way, they'd all know more before the night was over.

Mike joked with Parker and Alexis while they pulled on their bulletproof vests. They were only planning on knocking on a suspect's door tonight, but like everything at the Bureau, it came with procedures, precautions, and paperwork. Mike shrugged into his jacket, checked his weapon and looked at his watch for the time. It was past quitting time for most of the office staff, but most people weren't home in that part of town until after five and they only planned to knock once. They had information about the owner of the building but knew nothing about the tenant occupying the small greystone duplex. Alexis had spent part of the afternoon trying to determine who they were up against, but the appropriate paperwork hadn't been filed with the city. That was all the sniffing around any of them were willing to do before showing up. It was never a good idea to tip-off a suspect with something to hide.

An hour later, Mike led the way down a narrow entryway in the turn of the century building. While his partners were more than willing to take the lead, most people took Mike seriously from first impressions alone. Mike rapped his fist against the door. Nothing. Another knock. Scratching noises came from behind the door, but it still didn't open. Parker and Alexis stood on either side of him and they both began to move their hands closer to their weapons. Mike raised his hand for three more forceful bangs of his fist against the door. When the door creaked open, he wasn't prepared for who was behind it. A grandmotherly woman in a night coat peeked through a crack in the opening spanned by a locked chain. Looking for the source of the squeaking noise, Mike's eyes fell on a walker with tennis balls on the feet. Well, he didn't take this job for its predictability.

Mike asked some questions of the curious tenant—her name was Myrtle Moore, thank you very much for asking—and they confirmed she lived alone. After apologies for disturbing her this late in the evening and thanking her for her cooperation, the team beat a strategic retreat. Once the door to the greystone slammed shut behind them, Alexis let out a small sigh. Before she could say anything, Parker said, "I am not going to be the guy writing this one up."

Mike grumbled. "First time in my career I've been tempted to falsify paperwork."

Parker gave a wry grin. "Does a walker count as a weapon?" Alexis laughed, and Parker put his hand on her shoulder. "I vote Alex does the paperwork."

"Seconded." Mike said over his shoulder.

"Fine," Alexis said, "But I'm marking it top secret so we don't have to talk about this ever again." She sighed and pulled out her phone. "I guess I better tell Scarlett." Mike rubbed a hand down his face. The new profiler was going to hear about this—the same one who'd given him her blessing to investigate the armed and dangerous octogenarian. So much for starting off with a good first impression. At least they hadn't worn riot gear.

SIX

Scarlett Callahan slammed her foot into a heavy punching dummy in the FBI gym with a satisfying *thunk*. She repeated the motion a few more times, switched sides and delivered another roundhouse seconds later. It was a good thing her first meeting wasn't for another two hours. It was going to take more than a few hard kicks to chase the stress away today.

The charity had been hacked again last night. Her explicit approval of the investigation into the retiree *while the hack was in progress* was the cherry on top of it all. Finally, upon learning of these developments, the Special Agent in Charge decided to reallocate Mike Moretti's other assignments in order to fully dedicate him to her investigation. Which meant the S.A.C. thought she couldn't do her job. Lovely.

After the tops of her feet began to ache from the repeated impacts, she took a step back from the dummy and raised her fists, bouncing lightly on the balls of her feet as she alternated between jabs and punches. When she spun to chop the dummy's neck, she saw a familiar outline in the doorway.

"Hey, friend." Scarlett stepped away from the outlet of her frustration to pick her towel off the floor and wipe her face.

Alexis approached slowly with her hands raised in surrender, and Scarlett grinned before throwing the towel at her. Alexis snagged it out of the air. "You okay?"

Scarlett put her hands on her hips and nodded before looking away. "I will be."

"You couldn't have done anything to prevent the hack. And hey, at least you weren't there when we met Myrtle. She offered us cookies and tea if we wanted to stay for a while. Thanked us for our fine service to our country." Scarlett grimaced in response. "Oh, that's not helping. Too soon?"

Alexis slid her shoes off at the edge of the mat and picked up a pair of thick padded targets for her hands. She gestured to the pads. Scarlett alternated tapping them with her foot, lighter than she'd been kicking the dummy.

Alexis raised them slightly. "Again. Harder. Don't insult me by taking it easy."

Twenty minutes later, Scarlett felt like herself again. Well, she felt 80 percent like herself and 20 percent like a failure, which was at least an improvement. It was nice of Alexis to notice she was upset when they'd talked in the locker room this morning. Of course, venting about their investigation before storming over to the punching bags and dummies wasn't a subtle signal, but she appreciated it all the same.

"Thank you," Scarlett said. "I needed that."

"I suspected. You ready to talk about it?"

"Almost."

"It's not your fault, Scarlett." Alexis watched Scarlett's shoulders bunch up again. Scarlett had flown through her Ph.D. program and started working for the FBI at the age of twenty-four. Her unwillingness to admit defeat and overdeveloped sense of responsibility had contributed to her success but it came with its own sort of baggage. Not surprisingly, Scarlett was blaming herself for not being clairvoyant and had come in this morning to work off some of the frustration. It was a tactic Alexis herself employed. Nothing brought clarity to a tough case like pounding out five or six miles on a treadmill, which she planned to do just as soon as she got Scarlett back on track.

"I appreciate the support. It just sucks." Scarlett grabbed a curl that had escaped her ponytail and tucked it back behind her ear before pulling her leg up behind her in a stretch.

"Yeah, I know. But we'll figure it out." Alexis dropped a hand over her friend's shoulder and then made a face, theatrically wiping the sweat off her palm. Scarlett bumped Alexis with her hip and Alexis diverted to the treadmills, giving her a wave as she jogged over to the equipment to start her workout in earnest.

As Scarlett showered and got ready for her day, frustration and nervous energy trickled back into her psyche. All of the signs of distress she looked for when questioning a suspect manifested themselves in her without her permission. She kept rubbing her necklace absently and when she tried to smile, she didn't even have to look in the mirror to realize she wouldn't fool anyone. Scarlett had a meeting this morning to report out on the developments of her case with the Special Agent in Charge, the same agent who had informed her via 11 p.m. email that Agent Moretti would be helping her out full-time now. While Scarlett typically specialized in the unusual, this case was proving especially difficult to untangle on a short timeline. Their culprit remained stubbornly invisible, bleeding the charity of funds a little at a time.

Scarlett ran a hand through her damp hair and took a moment to make sure she was presentable before leaving the locker room. She was short and often mistaken for being younger, so she always took care to dress more nicely than the job required. Today, she was wearing a crisp gray button-down and black pencil skirt with sling back heels. She'd swapped out her contacts, necessary for working out, for her glasses, friendlier for staring at a screen all day. Her stylish frames brought a little personality to her professional clothing. A large white pearl necklace made her look older than nineteen...or at least that's what she told herself. A stop at the café in the bottom of the building armed her with much needed, drinkable coffee. While it seemed insufficient, she'd done everything she could to prepare herself to deliver a whole lot of bad news.

Mike Moretti thumped into his chair and turned on his computer. He was capable of brushing off the occasional inevitable dead end. It really wasn't a big deal. At all. He was just fighting crime, one old lady at a time. He ran a hand through his hair and turned his neck to crack it on each side. It was going to take a strong cup of coffee to get him moving today. While Mike dropped into the FBI field office regularly when he was working in the field, it didn't seem normal to be spending more of his time there just yet. He went into the small break area and poured some coffee into navy ceramic mug. He sniffed at it and grimaced before taking a long sip. He'd had worse.

Parker joined him moments later. "Hey, Mikey. Tough luck about last night." Mike grumbled into his mug in response. "No sulking, dude. Shit happens."

"I don't sulk."

Parker raised an eyebrow. "Hey, the evidence pointed to that apartment and you made a call. This guy even has Scarlett stumped. It's just a weird case, man."

Mike nodded and headed over to the large whiteboard in the common area they shared with a number of other agents. While Jordan's Silicon Valley techies would call their arrangement an open office, Mike called it, "the government is too cheap to splurge on walls."

Mike placed his coffee on Parker's desk and picked up a marker. He put a big "X" through the location they'd visited the night before. There were no pictures yet, just dates of when the charity had been hacked. He added the date of the previous evening to the list since he'd found that delightful update greeting him in his email this morning. The CEO was in the habit of paying the ransoms immediately to "minimize impact," which wasn't helping them catch the guy. Funny how he'd done that even after the FBI had gotten involved. He wrote the CEO's name in the center of the board. Mike stared at the information then picked up the file on Parker's desk. He didn't realize how long he'd been focusing on the evidence until he took a sip of cold coffee. After making a face, he felt a hand clap on his back.

"Hey, Mikey. How're you doing?" Alexis studied the whiteboard and crossed her arms.

"Fine," Mike said into his paperwork.

"Happens to everyone, Mikey. You're not special," Alexis said, cheekily.

Mike looked up from the stack of reports he was studying with a raised eyebrow. Alexis was a great agent, loved her job, and gave him endless shit. She was a good friend who deserved a complete sentence. "Yeah, I hate it when we get a smart one." While the FBI didn't get a lot easy wins, the vast majority of the cases they dealt with had at least one stupid mistake for them to exploit. Since that wasn't happening, they needed to step up their game. Alexis stood silently next to Mike, staring at the sparse whiteboard. She tapped the big black X on the board.

"Alright. I'm not getting anything. I'm going to check with Scarlett to see if anything new came in." Alexis turned on her heel and disappeared down a hallway. He'd do the same soon. Just as soon as he had some time to figure it out on his own.

Alexis knocked on Scarlett's door and her friend looked up from rubbing her face.

"None of that. I already unwound you once this morning. I can't keep up if you redo the damage faster than I undo it." Scarlett gave her a small smile and Alexis sat in her guest chair.

Scarlett grimaced. "It worked for a little while, but I had my meeting with the S.A.C. this morning. I had to explain why I haven't put together a decent profile on the perp who is extracting ransom from a highly-respected charity when I have three special agents and Jordan at my disposal. He was nice about it, but it feels unprofessional to be outsmarted while we're watching."

Alexis raised her eyebrows. "Or maybe we don't have enough to work with."

"I'm missing something. There's nothing worse than a criminal who thinks he—or she—is smarter than everyone else. Given the phrasing of the last two text messages, there is probably some personal connection. But we haven't uncovered anything solid yet."

"What else do we know?"

"Not much. There have been three separate attacks on the charity. Each time, they've paid an increasingly higher ransom and the total bill is now up to $70,000. They're finally letting Jordan sit with their team but his first impression is that this hack used a more sophisticated custom attack instead of off-the-shelf ransomware. World Partner's insurance is balking at the repeat offenses and the CEO is worried they're going to have to start paying him out of pocket. Jordan's trying to help them beef up their system but since they don't have a lot of clues, it's a slow process. They're a charity—why go after them when you could literally go anywhere else?"

Alexis decided it would be best not to mention that when she had questions like that, she usually went to Scarlett. "Well, does our perp know that he's going after a not-for-profit?"

"It's called the World Partners for Peace. I'd think if they were smart enough to hack the system, they're smart enough to figure out that they're sticking their hand in the offering plate, so to speak. That means that the perp either doesn't care, needs the money and has access, or has an axe to grind."

"Axe to grind seems unlikely for a charity."

"You'd think. But not everyone has a moral backbone. And beyond that, I'm providing no insight whatsoever."

"In your defense, we're not working off a lot of information here."

Scarlett picked up her laptop bag and gave Alexis an apologetic look. "Thank you. I really do appreciate it, but I need to catch up with Jordan. Then, I'm going to go spend some time with you guys and crack this case for real. Oh, and I should probably meet the additional agent the S.A.C. thought was necessary to help me solve this in person."

"You mean Mike. Is that what this is about?" Alexis crossed her arms.

Scarlett tightened her hand on the strap of her bag. "Look, I have nothing against Mike Moretti. I've never met the guy—we've only exchanged emails and he seems…fine. It's not a big deal. I just hate that we've had to pull someone in from the field full-time because I can't figure it out." Alexis started to defend her, but Scarlett raised a hand. "You're going to tell me that it's not my fault, which I appreciate, and I'm going to pretend I believe you, because if I don't, I'll be late to my meeting with Jordan. I'll stop by the whiteboard after. Then, let's see if we can put our heads together and finally crack this thing."

SEVEN

Mike thumbed through the evidence in the slim manila file folder on his desk. He put the folder down to add another detail to his notes on the communal white board and heard light footsteps behind him. A young woman with funky glasses and curly red hair walked up and stood beside him without preamble. She radiated energy and focus. She was obviously an intern. Now he had no leads and had to babysit an intern. Awesome. He gave her a silent nod, but instead of taking the hint that he didn't have time right now, she continued to stare at the board. He asked, "So, you helping with this case?"

"Yep. The S.A.C. wants another update from me soon." Oh great, the Special Agent in Charge himself had hired this one. He crossed his arms and hoped she'd get bored, but instead, she sat down on the desk in front of the whiteboard like she owned the place. Okay, she had some guts. One point for the intern.

"Anything new?" she asked.

"Are you up to date?" Mike asked. Sandy, his unit chief, had explicitly told Mike he wanted him mentoring new agents and Mike had agreed that, in theory, it was a fair request. Everyone had to start somewhere and the intern had made herself comfortable. At least she could make herself useful.

The intern scrunched her nose at him and gave him a strange look. "Yes. I've been helping with the investigation since day one. The only thing that's consistent is that there isn't a pattern between strikes. The first one was fifteen days ago in the early morning, the next one was five days ago in the late evening, and the last one was yesterday evening. Why the difference?"

"What if it's a team?" Mike had refreshed his coffee, which had taken it from undrinkable to mediocre. He took a sip. He wasn't dumb enough to turn away help on a tough case and the intern seemed competent.

"Possible but unlikely."

Mike raised his eyebrows and she gestured at the board, as she explained her logic. "Hackers can work in teams but this person is likely working independently. Our tech team is excellent. They haven't found the source of the breach, which would be harder to conceal if there were several people working together. Once you get more people involved, they start leaving evidence behind when they coordinate. No, to be this invisible it's likely one person implementing the hack. Two at most, but only one doing the dirty work."

"Not bad." Mike said. The intern was helpful. Duly noted. "So how are they hiding?"

"Don't know. I just came from talking to Jordan. He's convinced someone on the inside is involved. But everyone has a unique login and their actions are traceable once they log in to their work computers. It's a security feature for the benefactors of the charity as much as for the charity itself. They may serve the greater good, but it's still a lot of money changing hands."

"Do they have to log in to do this kind of damage?"

"Well, I would assume so." She winced. "Damn. That's the problem. I assumed. Mike, good work." She tapped her hand against her leg before leaping to her feet and clapping him on the back. Mike raised an eyebrow, but she had already gathered up her laptop bag and waved behind her as she power-walked away.

Alone again, Mike began to assemble a series of pictures on the board. The intern made a good point—there was a lot of money changing hands. And Martín Vásquez, the CEO, was his top suspect.

Martín Vásquez had hidden evidence until he was forced to share it and paid quickly, before they could get the information they needed. That sort of thing couldn't be dismissed out of hand. Plus, the ominous text messages, albeit brief, may have been his version of a CYA.

A handful of the IT people that Parker thought could be involved were waiting in the wings to be compared against the profile that Scarlett was putting together, just in case it wasn't Martín. He listed their names on a far corner of the board. After some thought, he wrote Jen Duncan, the accountant with the weird behavior, in another corner of the whiteboard. They had no reason to suspect her, but with so little to go on, it wouldn't hurt to write her name down. She could have seen something and not wanted to get anyone in trouble. He began to make a list of character traits of the CEO and it evolved into a complex web of motive, time, and place over the next hour. He took a step back to take in the full web of information and just about knocked over the intern, who nimbly stepped out of his path.

"Hey again." She gestured to the board. "Good job summing up the evidence, but you've got the wrong guy."

"Excuse me?" Mike placed his whiteboard marker back in its tray and turned to face her with his arms crossed. She was a full foot shorter than he was, and she looked up to meet his eyes.

"The CEO is in the center of your web, which means you think he's important. It's not the CEO. I talked to him, ran a background check, made an assessment. It's not him."

"Really? When did you talk to him?"

"I set up a meeting Monday and did the research both before and after. His finances are solid and he has no history of this type of thing. Moreover, no motive. Messages sent to him simply cannot be traced back to him. Final death knell is his knowledge of the subject matter. If Jordan can't figure out this hack, the average Joe can't do it either. He may be smart enough to run a major charity but when it comes to code, Martín Vásquez is unequivocally the average Joe. He can install his own software but that's about it. Until we have evidence that implicates him in a larger plot, we're better off focusing on the charity staff with access, ability and motive."

Mike whistled. He walked up to the whiteboard, erased Martín's name, and moved his photo to the side of the board. He raised an eyebrow and tossed her the marker. "Okay, your turn."

Scarlett caught the marker easily. The look on Mike Moretti's face after telling him he was wrong was both priceless and a bit of a surprise. Instead of getting annoyed with her intrusion, he backed down in the face of sound logic to give her a turn to whack at the intellectual piñata. He had a reputation as a tough guy but underneath, he was solid. The reasons Alexis and Parker liked him so much were starting to come into focus.

Scarlett walked past him and uncapped the marker. Raising it to the board, she narrated, "Our mastermind is a coding expert or is working with someone who has the knowledge. Here's the tricky part—the best motives I've come up with are: someone who has something to prove or a bone to pick or someone who needs the money and is reluctant to take more than they need."

"How do you figure?"

"The amount of money involved. The charity has an insurance policy that will cover a bigger breach than this. If they have enough inside knowledge to hack, it's probable they know the scale of the operation, which is well beyond the 70 thousand dollars they've asked for. Therefore, greed isn't the only factor. Money is involved, obviously, but there is another layer to this we'll miss if we just focus on the ransom. My gut says there's inexperience at play here too."

"Why?"

"They've done this three times instead of one. Repeating the same crime in the same location is a great way to get caught. One and done is the best way to do it. They're playing with fire and upping the possibility of criminal charges each time they strike."

"Can't argue with any of that. Look, you've got a head for this sort of thing. You should come with us the next time we go out to the charity. It'd be a good learning experience for you."

Scarlett raised an eyebrow. "I could do that, I guess."

"I'd recommend it. You've got potential. You should talk to our profiler. I haven't met her in person, but everyone thinks she's pretty smart."

Scarlett mouth quirked as realization dawned. "Oh yeah? What else can you tell me about this profiler?"

Mike shrugged. "I'm told she doesn't miss much and she doesn't suffer fools."

Scarlett let out a belly laugh. "You could say that. It just became apparent that I never introduced myself. I'm Scarlett Callahan. It's nice to meet you."

Mike scratched his forehead and gave her a wry grin. "Ah, *the* Dr. Scarlett Callahan. Not an intern?" Scarlett shook her head and Alexis, who had previously been working at her desk and pretending not to eavesdrop, slapped a hand over her mouth. Mike turned around and shot her a look. She crossed her arms and leaned back in her chair to watch the show.

"Not even close. I will take you up on your offer, though. I'd like to get a little closer to this case." Mike rubbed a hand through his hair and the big, tough guy even managed to look a little sheepish.

The sound of a throat clearing behind her made Scarlett jump. "Hey guys." Jordan held a piece of paper in one hand while the other remained in his front sweatshirt pocket. "Thought you might want to see this."

Parker and Alexis rose to join them but Scarlett snagged the paper out of Jordan's hand first. "Whoa. You left the programmer's cave to bring it to us. Must be important." Scarlett studied it and beamed. "You got it. Nice work Jordan."

"Explain?" Alexis said, craning her neck to read over Scarlett's shoulder. Scarlett gave her the print out. "Mike and I chatted earlier—thank you, Mike—and I realized something. We had the charity check every computer login and history of each employee and there was no trace of a hack. Jordan's just been plugging the holes he can find, hoping he's fixing the right one."

Mike leaned against a table. "Couldn't it have come from outside?"

Scarlett pointed at the paper. "You'd think so. But Jordan couldn't find a way in. They keep their system on a sort of lockdown with really limited access if you aren't physically on-site or don't have a company computer. Getting access to the right computers is easiest to do on-site. Small problem, though. The records from the controlled computers were reviewed and we didn't find anything. But that's not the good part. The good part is that there is a visitor computer where every single person who comes into the charity to volunteer or visit has to log in."

Parker crossed his arms. "And that one isn't under the same rules as the rest of the network."

"Because they wanted to make it easy for visitors to sign in," Scarlett said.

Jordan nodded. "Exactly. It's not a great set-up but it's not the first time I've seen it. The guest computer is connected to the network, which gave our hacker access."

Scarlett smiled. "Bingo."

"Nice work, you guys," Mike said. "That's something we can work with. What's next, Jordan?"

Jordan smiled. "It's already done. Their IT team upped the security on the visitor computer. And now I know where to go looking for the malicious code."

Scarlett raised an eyebrow. "You are going to go home tonight, right, Jordan?"

Jordan laughed. "On a case like this? No promises."

EIGHT

S everal miles from the FBI Chicago field office, a hacker opened a door to check the hallway before getting to work. She'd already unleashed three successful attacks, but the rules of the game required that she keep hacking until she got caught or she couldn't find any more ways in. She'd been sloppy in covering up her location for the first hack, but each subsequent time, she'd been just a little more careful. The "money" she demanded went to the dummy account Martín suggested in his instructions, and he did a great job acting like he was genuinely afraid in his replies to her company phone. He was a good guy, totally having fun with the task at hand, even though she was just an intern. Of course, he could just appreciate her offbeat sense of humor. Footsteps nearby warned her that her time was almost up. She needed just one more minute…and it was done. The footsteps got closer and she shut down the visitor's workstation before throwing her laptop bag over her shoulder. And people assumed her internship was all busy work.

Emma placed a hand on the exit door, heart pounding. She'd been eager to prove herself here, so much so that her task actually made her feel like she was doing something wrong, instead of helping. She jumped at Barbara's voice right behind her. "Emma, honey, what are you doing here so late?" Barbara rested a motherly hand on her shoulder. "Your parents will be worried sick."

Emma gave a soft smile to the woman who was more like family to her than a friend. There were a lot of things going wrong in her life, but the people and work of the charity kept her going. She couldn't cure cancer, but she could use the determination that had gotten her through chemo to help other people. She was under strict instructions to keep the ransomware simulation confidential, and truthfully, it had been fun to play along. Fortunately, there was no surveillance camera over the visitor's computer or someone might have caught her in real life. That would be more embarrassing then getting caught virtually. "Hi, Miss Barb. I'm actually just leaving."

Barbara smiled. "Not only are you our most loyal volunteer, I can say with confidence you are the most meticulous. If the way you manage our website is any indication, you'll be a force to be reckoned with in the software field. I think you have a bright future ahead of you, Emma."

Tears came to Emma's eyes. During her treatment, she studied and coded whenever she had the energy, even from her hospital bed. Getting lost in the numbers had kept her alive. And now, it was finally doing someone some good.

"Gotcha." Mike grinned at the message that greeted him when he arrived at work the following morning. Score one for the good guys. They'd finally plugged their hole, and not a minute too soon. Martín Vásquez received another threatening text message last night. Per Jordan's instructions, he logged in, confirmed the system was still up and running, and called the FBI instead of paying off his hacker.

Given the positive progress, Mike decided he had a little time to spend in the gym before the day really got started. The FBI allocated work time for keeping in shape, due to the strict physical requirements of an agent's job. If he was going to spend more time in the office, he could at least take advantage of the facilities. He'd started with free weights and was getting ready to hit the treadmills when he saw a small woman with curly red hair beating the bejesus out of a punching dummy. He chuckled. Maybe there was a reason they got along. His time working undercover had taught him flexibility and he diverted from his planned activity to satisfy his curiosity. Mike slipped off his shoes before walking on the mat. To his surprise, Scarlett turned from the punching dummy and greeted him with a wide smile. She tossed him a set of protective gear, and he accepted the unspoken challenge.

Once again, Mike Moretti surprised her. Instead of treating her with kid gloves, he met Scarlett kick for kick, his strength an even match for her speed. A quick tap to the pad on his arms with her toes and the game was on.

"Where'd you learn how to do this?" Mike asked, ducking away from her foot and nearly catching it before she pulled it away. She bounced on her toes as they circled one another.

"Where do you think? The dojo."

"Why?"

"Why not?" While they didn't experience the same level of danger as field agents, analysts didn't always just sit in the office. Like everything else in her life, Scarlett had come into her career prepared for anything that might get thrown at her. Figuratively or literally.

Mike grinned and tried to close in on her, but she ducked away. "Fair enough. You must have heard the good news or you wouldn't be taking it so easy on me. You find out anything else out about the case?" Scarlett paused a second too long and Mike tapped her on the stomach with a controlled side kick.

She narrowed her eyes at him. "That's not fighting fair."

"It wasn't unfair. Plus, it was a light tap."

"How sweet. My hero," Scarlett said, batting her eyelashes. However, she didn't quite manage to keep the smile off her face. He was a smartass but he wasn't a jerk. She kept her weight on the balls of her feet and delivered some punches and elbows to the air around Mike's chest. She hadn't had this much fun working out in a long time. "Jordan said he wanted to talk in person. I set up a meeting for an hour from now." When Mike paused to process the information, Scarlett took a swipe at Mike's stomach. He grabbed her hand to stop it, just as she'd hoped he would, and she whirled into him, throwing her weight into his stomach and staying low, sweeping his feet with her legs. He landed on the soft mat with a huge grin.

"Now, Dr. Callahan. *That* wasn't fighting fair."

"Since you can hold your own, you can call me Scarlett. And I never promised to fight fair." Scarlett grinned and offered a hand up, which Mike took. She often saw the worst side of human nature and was generally wary around new people. It was clear why Mike didn't elicit that response. He had zero brain-to-mouth filter and he was a straight arrow. Maybe it wouldn't be so bad to have him on her team after all.

Apparently, the special agent felt the same way about her. Mike gave her a fist bump when he got to his feet. "You're alright, Scarlett. You're alright."

NINE

"Hey Grandma, can I get you another cup of tea?" Emma Moore leaned over to kiss her grandma's cheek and pick up her empty cup. Even while her friends moved in a slow trickle into assisted living, Myrtle Moore had stayed independent, due in no small part to her keen intelligence and plain old stubbornness.

"No, thank you, honey." Myrtle patted her granddaughter's hand. "How are your folks doing?"

Emma looked at her hands. "They're doing well."

"And your daddy? That boy sure carries a lot of worry around on his shoulders."

Emma swallowed. "He's getting by. I wish it hadn't...I wish I hadn't..."

"Oh, hush. Not a lick of this was your fault, and we couldn't be prouder of you. With your heart and your strength, Miss Emma, you'll move mountains. They'll figure this out." Grandma Myrtle gave her a wink and Emma's smile faltered. "Honey, are you okay?"

"Yeah. Just worried about Mom and Dad." Emma kept it short. Her dad, the rock of their family, had been careful to hide their problems from the formidable Myrtle Moore. She'd give you her last penny and wouldn't let you say a word about it while she starved to death with a smile on her face. Emma's family was drowning in medical bills from her cancer treatment. Her dad had swallowed his pride and accepted a small amount of help from the hospital. Nothing made you feel poorer than accepting a handout. Especially when the handout hadn't been enough. However, her Aunt Jen was an accountant and had recently stepped in to help her mother manage the bills. After a stressful few weeks, Aunt Jen announced that she'd figured it out and it was going to be okay. Her mom and dad weren't fully convinced, and the stress of the situation hung in the area like a heavy fog at home.

Emma looked over at her grandma's computer. It was a reminder of the good in the world. World Partners for Peace had sponsored her support group and provided her with personal necessities during her treatment. Working at World Partners had allowed her to give back, even just a little bit, for what she'd been given. Using her grandma's computer to send the first message to Mr. Vásquez had been a risk to her credibility, but no one had figured her out. She'd have to write that one up for the security team. Martín Vásquez had a lot of confidence in his IT team but some of it was misplaced. Well, not all of it. They hadn't left many holes for her to exploit. Since her last attack had been a dud, she needed to go home and do more research to see if she could pull some new tricks out of her hat. Her worry slipped away into a genuine smile. She gave her grandmother a hug goodbye and went back to home to try and hack World Partners for Peace one more time.

As far FBI cybercrime analysts went, Jordan Sykes was a little unconventional. By the age of twenty-two, he had learned to code, finished college and formed his own software company. After less than a decade in the tech industry, he had all the money he could imagine needing for a lifetime. Good thing, because his FBI paycheck wasn't quite as lucrative as the one from his last job. However, his job catching cybercriminals at the FBI was a lot more fun than convincing venture capitalists he knew what he was talking about. Especially on days like today.

A check of his watch told him it was time to move along to the meeting he'd called in Scarlett's office. Her office was large by Bureau standards, but it was more cramped than his at home. He scratched at his two days of beard growth and paused to put a reminder to shave on his phone. It would go off tomorrow morning before work, and with any luck, he'd be sleeping at home tonight.

Alexis high-fived him on the way in and Scarlett gave him a quiet nod. She leaned against her desk but didn't sit. Parker and Mike filled one of the small couches in Scarlett's stylish make-shift sitting area. Scarlett had an eye for beautiful pieces. Since her work largely revolved around observing details, it didn't come as a surprise she knew which items would work well together.

When Jordan realized everyone was staring at him, he began. "So, I found something interesting."

Mike raised an eyebrow. "We assumed."

"I think what Mr. Personality is asking is, what did you find?" Alexis asked.

"I figured out how they locked down the system. Once I spent some time with the records from the visitor's computer, it was obvious. The reason I couldn't figure out how they locked down the network is because it never happened."

Scarlett stood. "I'm sorry?"

"It was beautifully fabricated." Scarlett raised an eyebrow and Jordan continued. "Smoke and mirrors for the 21st century. Have you ever done the thing where you screenshot someone's desktop and set it as their background to make it look like the files are still there but then hide them somewhere else? That way when they try and click on an icon, nothing opens?"

"Jordan, I'm starting to think there is a reason we don't let you out of the back room," Alexis said.

Jordan grinned. "Be nice to the software guy. I have plenty more tricks up my sleeve and that's grade school stuff. But go with me on this. At my company, my software engineers did stuff like this to each other all the time. Some poor schmuck would leave his computer unlocked and the rest was history. Extremely low tech but remarkably effective to someone who'd never been a mark before."

Parker crossed his arms. "And this relates to the case?"

"Yes," Jordan said. "Our bad guy is using smoke and mirrors. Note that he only ever contacted the CEO directly. We couldn't find evidence that he'd penetrated the entire network because he didn't have to. It would have exposed him to unnecessary risk. We couldn't find him because we were looking in the wrong place."

"I thought you found a security hole?" Scarlett said.

"I found several. But our hacker didn't use any of them. They did a neat trick where they set up phony screens and when our CEO was 'locked out,' he believed the whole system was down. The text messages scared him into acting before checking with his team."

"But the money is real." Parker said.

"Very real," Scarlett said. "We've confirmed that the transfers occurred."

Parker let out a low whistle. "Does that help us find our guy?"

"It might," Scarlett said. "Jordan, is it easier to hack into the CEO's computer than it is the rest of the network?"

Jordan paused for a moment, trying to translate his world into what the agents would consider plain English. "Not necessarily. It's just a different location. But, if the hacker threatens to shut down the whole charity, I'm a lot more confident he can't make good on it. Especially now that we've closed the gates, so to speak."

"How confident?"

Jordan scratched his chin. "Nothing is 100 percent. But with that hole closed, I think we should see if Mr. Vásquez is willing to play chicken."

Mike tilted his head towards Scarlett. "You're the one who's good at figuring out what nutcases are going to do next. Should Martín Vásquez play chicken?"

Scarlett raised an eyebrow. "Filter, Mike, filter." Her tone was neutral but her eyes gave away her amusement.

"I'm used to it," Jordan chimed in. "Can't you just run the financials on everyone at the charity?"

Scarlett sat behind her desk and leaned back in her chair. "Not really. Probable cause and warrants get ugly if we look at everyone's personal information. Especially if we've mitigated the immediate risk. We're still trying to trace the money through the cryptocurrency site they used but they've covered their tracks pretty well. Did you guys learn anything more about the people you flagged?"

"Nothing turned up in our searches. The IT guy seems clean, but he's got the most to hide. I'd like some more time with him." Parker scratched his chin.

"I'd like to talk to Jen again," Mike said. "I think she knows more than she's letting on."

"Alex, your ladder climber?" Scarlett said.

Alexis scrunched up her face. "Ah, I have no idea. Not a bad idea to talk to him. Can we get some interviews set up with them without spooking them?"

Mike looked at Scarlett. "Crazypants expert—what do you think?"

Scarlett shook her head at him. "I think crazypants is an assumption I'm unwilling to make at this time. Interviews, however, are a good idea. I'll see if I can talk Martín into it. And I'll see if he's willing to push back harder on our hacker if they try again."

"Still think Martín isn't a part of this?" Mike asked.

"Probably not. But we'll have him close by, just in case. Let's get this one wrapped up, guys."

The team exited the small office and Mike leaned against the door while Scarlett made a phone call. Her tone was polite but urgent, and the following day's interviews were set up within minutes.

"Want to do anything else to spook our criminal?" Mike asked, and Scarlett steepled her hands, tapping her fingers together.

"Good question. With the text message threats, we need to be careful about which buttons we push. We could set up some extra surveillance for the lobby if we're sure they're only using that computer or give Martín a script for the next time our hacker makes contact. Good idea, Mike."

"Yeah. Not sure if it's a good idea to encourage you to mess with people's minds." Mike grinned.

"Anything else, Mike?"

"Nah." He winked and she didn't quite hide her smile as he left.

TEN

Emma hunched over her keyboard in the nearly-empty World Partners for Peace office. After her last failed attempt, she didn't have many tricks left to get into Martín's system without leaving tracks. Since it was her last planned strike, she'd decided to take a risk and enter the system through her work computer when there weren't many people around. She had one last idea for bluffing him with a new login screen and error message. Her actions would be traceable by IT this time, so she'd saved this one for last. A few quick strokes of the keyboard and it was done. She sent out a text message and waited.

Less than a minute later, her work cell phone pinged. *Not this time. We know who you are.* It had a creepy horror movie vibe and Emma laughed. At least they were having fun with it. She pulled up Martín's number and thought carefully before typing back. *Oh, you know who I am? I'm watching you right now.* Pausing, she decided to add just a little more drama and chuckled. Not every intern was lucky enough to get to work so closely with the CEO, even via text message. *This. Isn't. Over.* Only it was. Martín didn't bite on the new login screen, which meant he knew it was a fake. And she couldn't find another way in. Sighing, she pulled up her security report and added the last details. She saved the document but wanted to wait another day or two to perfect it before she sent the final version. It wasn't every day she'd get this kind of opportunity, and she didn't want to blow it. On top of being a smart guy, Martín was a good person. And apparently shared her wicked sense of humor. She shut down her system and went home. Well, check and mate. As she laid in bed that evening, she sent a quick message to her aunt.

Can't get in. Out of ideas. Hope it helped u.

A few bubbles appeared while she waited.

Good job, Em. Proud of you.

Job well done, she laid her head back against the pillow and drifted off to sleep. It was safe to say her chemo brain had gone into full retreat. It was nice to get back to living her life where she'd left off.

The following morning, Mike, Parker and Alexis bantered with one another while waiting for Scarlett. Their interviews at World Partners for Peace were scheduled for the mid-morning and they planned to travel as a group. Mike came up short when Scarlett arrived and handed them each a piece of paper detailing the latest threats.

Mike rubbed a hand down his face. "Shit. This just escalated. Someone tell Martín to make sure he has extra security around?"

"Thought that was us," Parker quipped at the same time Scarlett nodded.

"Everyone have their weapons?" Mike looked around and each agent lifted their suit jacket. When Scarlett did nothing, he said, "Is the intern going in unarmed?"

Scarlett lifted her pant leg. On it was a smaller version of the standard issue Glock the rest of them were carrying. "I've never had to use it, but I'm trained. Under the circumstances, it seemed like a good idea."

"Well, don't hurt yourself in there," Mike said, forgetting for a moment they had an audience. Great, he was going to get all kinds of shit for going soft on their profiler. So what? Even if she outranked him, she still wasn't that familiar with fieldwork. He cleared his throat and stood a little taller. "Alright, guys. Here's the plan. We go in and say we are completing informational interviews. Parker, your guy is first. Then Alexis' pick. Then I'm going to see what I can glean out of Jen."

"Whoa, take it easy on the details, Moretti. Not sure I can keep all of that straight," Scarlett said with a cheeky grin.

"What? The rest is here in your reports." He pointed at Parker and Alexis. "You guys need a refresher course? No? Okay. Let's do this. Oh, and be on the lookout. Our suspect may know something is up. I don't want to fill out the paperwork if you guys get shot." There. That was something they expected from him.

The check-in at World Partners for Peace was similar to the last time Scarlett had visited, with one notable exception. Martín Vásquez was there to greet her and her fellow agents at the door. Scarlett shook his very sweaty palm. She leaned in while she shook his hand. "It's okay. You're perfectly safe. We're all armed. Just stay close, and we'll be right here if anything happens." Instead of relaxing, he froze in place. Great. She'd elicited a deer in the headlights response. Maybe Mike was right to offer her the opportunity to practice her undercover work.

Alexis stepped forward and guided him towards the larger office area without him noticing that he was being shepherded. Well done, Alex. Inside of ten minutes, they were seated at a conference room table. Pete Smythe had been called to the conference room first. "This was the IT director who didn't mention the breach," Parker explained. "We just need to find out if he's hiding something."

Pete poked his head in the door and paused for a moment before slowly pushing it open, scanning the room. He shook each of their hands but his eyes remained on Martín.

"Mr. Vásquez, am I getting fired?"

"No, Pete. We just want to ask you some questions about your day-to-day job. The team thought it'd be good for me to learn alongside them." Martín's voice was calm and nonchalant. Good job, Martín. He recited his lines perfectly.

"Is this because I didn't catch the hacker? I...I wasn't shirking on the job. I didn't know there was a vulnerability. We just have a complex system..."

"Easy, Pete. We're not here to blame you. We just want to understand how complicated the work is to get you some help if you need it," Scarlett lied smoothly, but Mike had seen and heard everything he needed to know. Liars often kept it short and simple while trying to redirect the line of questioning. This guy was practically confessing to something he didn't do. And there was zero animosity towards Martín. Since he'd been the point of contact, there should be...something. He gave the team ten minutes for their questions. When it was still clear Pete wasn't their guy, Mike hit the metaphorical big red button.

"You weren't behind the hack, were you, Pete?" Mike asked, without preamble.

Pete's jaw dropped and he raised his arms in the air. "Are you kidding me? Do you think I would even consider doing that? I'm sorry, but how long have you known me? Five minutes? I don't care who you work for but I won't stand here and be accused of lying, cheating, and stealing from this organization. I have dedicated my life to this place and you just dropped in. Look through my computers, my house, my car. I don't have anything to hide."

Mike raised his hands. "Sorry, Pete. I had to ask."

"I'm sorry, Pete. Let's continue this conversation outside." Martín Vásquez rose, glared at Mike and mouthed, "*I'm going to do some damage control.*"

As the door closed behind Martín, Alexis lifted an eyebrow. "Going for subtle?"

Scarlett answered before he could. "Large hand gestures. Excessive explanation. Normal speech patterns. He's not behind this. Good job, Mike. Poor Mr. Vásquez has some work to do but we can cross him off our list."

Mike was speechless. He'd just assumed everyone would be annoyed that he was doing the wrong thing for the right reason and was prepared to face the consequences. Apparently, Scarlett agreed that they didn't have time to mess around if the CEO was facing a death threat. Alexis rolled her eyes. Parker chuckled and said, "Oh great, now there's two of you."

Scarlett and Mike laughed. Mike shrugged. "It worked."

A few minutes later, they began the process again. This time with Alexis' suck-up, Nick Burket. When he entered the room, he made a beeline for Alexis and held her hand just a second longer than everyone else's while staring at her eyes, then her…shirt. When they asked him introductory small-talk questions, he directed his answers to Alexis with a smooth smile. Oh, this one wasn't guilty, but it was funny. Mr. Burket wasn't sucking up because she was a consultant who might fire him. He had the hots for Alexis. On second thought, he could have the hots for Alexis and still be their hacker. That would be less funny.

Scarlett looked up from taking notes on the discussion and said, "Nick. What do you know about computers?"

"Oh, I know a lot about computers. Use them all the time in this line of work." He winked at Alexis. Mike choked back a laugh and Alexis finally caught on. He was proud of her self-control—she waited until Nick was talking to Scarlett to kick Mike under the table. Martín Vásquez came back into the room, took his seat, and gave Nick a nod. Nick sat up a little straighter.

Scarlett said, "Do you ever write your own code, apps, or software?"

Nick raised a questioning eyebrow. "No, but I'm willing to learn." He directed his answer to Alexis before his eyes flicked over to Martín. "Mr. Vásquez, are these people trying to fire me?"

"Why does everyone keep asking that?" Martín threw his hands in the air. "No, Nick. We're just trying to learn more about what everyone is doing here at the charity so that we can use our funds appropriately."

"See, that sounds like code for getting fired. And I'm way too valuable to the organization."

"Do you have a reason for me to fire you, Nick?" Martín asked, arms crossed. Martín was way off script, and Scarlett's eyes widened. Unlike Mike's calculated strike at Pete, Martín's approach and tone were scaring someone who hadn't been crossed off the suspect list just yet.

Nick sat up straight. "No, sir."

"Any grudges against me you want to talk about?" Okay. Time to reign in their CEO-turned-interrogator.

"No, sir." Nick's eyes went wide and his voice rose. He began to play with his tie and his body shifted away from Martín.

Scarlett rose and stuck out her hand. "Nick, thank you for your time. I think that's all we have for you right now. And you still have a job. We'll call you if we need you again." As Nick exited the room. Scarlett let out a big breath. "That was close. Classic signs of distress. Keep the red flag on that guy just in case."

"So he did it? Why'd you let him leave?" Martín said. He'd half-risen from his seat, his hands were on the table and he looked ready to punch someone or run.

"Easy there, cowboy," Mike said, placing a hand on his shoulder. "He may have just been uncomfortable. And Jordan, our IT guy, is watching your systems while we're here. He'll keep an eye on him."

Alexis looked at the sheet. "Jen's up next. Let's see what she knows about Nick."

Scarlett tapped her pen on the table while they waited for Jen to arrive. The longer they stayed in the conference room, the more warning they gave their unknown subject that someone was sniffing around. The IT guys all checked out and none of them seemed to fit the bill. They'd have to go back to the drawing board. Again. Scarlett had missed something. They'd all missed something. Well, so far, Mike had been on point. Maybe he was going to pull a rabbit of his hat with the last interview. She'd keep an open mind and have a back-up plan. Mike was whispering quietly to Martín, who put his hands in the air in surrender before crossing them and going silent. A shadow outside the conference room gave her enough warning to shake her head at Mike, who shook hands with Martín and then took his seat.

A soft tap at the door was followed by the entrance of a quiet, professional woman. Her mannerisms were small, almost timid, but her back was straight. According to Alexis' research, Jen Duncan was a single woman in her 30s who had recently donated some of her own salary back into the organization. Hardly the type of behavior one would expect of a hacker stealing from a charity. Still, Jen the accountant had a lot of access to sensitive financial information so perhaps she knew more than she was letting on. Women lied most frequently to protect someone else. Maybe a hacker boyfriend? Scarlett kept her careful smile in place as she shook Jen's damp hand and her mind raced through the possibilities. Martín's manner shifted 180 degrees from their last interview. His accusatory glare had disappeared and upon noticing Jen's nervous disposition, he moved to the other side of the conference table to sit beside her.

"Did I do something wrong?" Jen asked.

"I don't think so," Alexis said at the same time Martín said, "No."

Alexis continued. "We're just hoping to ask you a few questions about the selection process you manage for the charity donations." It was a question they'd planned in advance. A slam-dunk question intended to put her at ease before they asked the hard ones. However, she froze before carefully moving her hands to fiddle with her necklace. She was definitely hiding something.

Jen cleared her throat. "Of course. We have a procedure and a scoring system that we use to rank donor opportunities. There are some exceptions, of course, based on extraordinary circumstances."

"Such as?" Scarlett asked. She pulled out a pen and notebook as if to take notes. Jen shared a look with Martín. What was that about?

Jen's voice trembled. "I...I have to go. I can't do this." She stood up from her chair abruptly and a tear ran down her cheek.

"Jen, wait." Martín Vásquez stood and placed a hand on her arm. She shook it off and power walked out of the conference room. When Martín began to follow, he found Mike blocking his path.

"Why don't you have a seat, Mr. Vásquez. I think we have some time." Martín Vásquez rubbed his forehead, and Mike said calmly, "Is there something you aren't telling us about you and Ms. Duncan?"

Martín swallowed. "Nothing of interest to the FBI."

"Why don't you let us decide if a romantic relationship is of interest to us, Mr. Vásquez?" Alexis' tone was steady and direct.

"What? No. Absolutely not. I'm a happily married man twenty years her senior. She's become a very good friend of mine. I would never." Scarlett leaned back and crossed her arms. If Mr. Vásquez was going to dig himself into a hole, she wasn't about to stop him. He rubbed his forehead and closed his eyes. "Jen is a wonderful employee. She's as objective as you can be in this type of business, which is something I appreciate a great deal. Until recently. See, she had a family member who needed assistance, and as much as I would have liked to help her through the foundation, we turned her away."

"That's a little harsh," Alexis said.

"I understand it seems that way. But there's a reason we have a policy. If I make exceptions for one employee, it would set a bad precedent. We don't want people to believe you have to know someone who works here to receive a donation. I forwarded the case to a friend of mine at another charity. Her family member's case is being reviewed but due to the sensitive nature of the case, I'm not allowed to share any information with her until they make a decision. If the family member hadn't been related to Jen, they likely would have received the donation from us already. She's angry with me that working here counted against someone in need. We've been friends since she started here nearly ten years ago. This is affecting our friendship and it's been a challenging time for both of us."

"So you believe she's still mad at you?" Scarlett asked, not looking up from her notes.

"I refuse to answer any questions that will incriminate my friend. She wouldn't steal from me. Period."

Mike held up a form from the insurance company. "She didn't steal from you. In fact, isn't it true that as a senior accountant, she's one of the few people at the company that knew World Partners for Peace had insurance coverage for a cyberattack?"

Martín leaned in towards the agents and folded his hands on the table. His voice was softer now. "But, she doesn't know how to hack into our systems. You said yourself, it was sophisticated. If you want to find someone who could do this sort of thing, you'd be better off accusing Emma. She's a better programmer than some of my IT staff and she's only sixteen. You might as well point to our high schooler as your criminal mastermind."

Alexis skimmed the list of employees. "Emma Moore? You mean Jen's niece? Who recently faced a mountain of medical bills from fighting cancer? The Moore family wasn't the one you turned down, was it?"

"Aw, hell."

It was hard to say who moved first, but Scarlett was closest to the door and led the group out of the conference room, closely followed by Mike. Emma's desk was near the conference room and was hard to miss with the "Intrepid Interns" sign above it. Emma was sliding a backpack on her shoulders while Jen's head darted.

"Don't see a gun," Mike whispered under his breath, just loud enough for Scarlett to hear.

"Keep looking, Mike." Jen's eyes were wild when they met Scarlett's, and she used her hand to place Emma behind her, like a mama bear standing in front of her cub. Emma peeked around Jen but there was no fear in her eyes, only curiosity and confusion.

"Jen. We need you to come with us."

"Not happening."

Emma's eyebrows shot up at Jen's anger. "Auntie Jen!"

Jen kept one arm extended and her eyes darted, looking for something. Scarlett watched her carefully. Desperation was a dangerous thing and Auntie Jen was throwing up some major red flags. Jen darted through a small gap between the cubicles, followed by Emma shouting after her. Scarlett was small enough to squeeze through the gap and she followed the two women. The others ran around the outside but she had a few seconds head start—enough to head off...something. Jen ran towards the entrance and fumbled her bag. When she dropped it, Emma bent to pick it up.

Scarlett ran around her and said over her shoulder, "Stay here, Emma!"

"I can help!" Emma shouted. Scarlett bit back her frustration and kept running. Parker and Mike were close behind her and would have to handle Emma. Her professional opinion was that Emma wasn't a threat and if she was wrong, Scarlett was the one with her back to the potentially dangerous sixteen-year-old. If she slowed down, Jen would be on the loose doing God knows what. Scarlett reached the stairwell just as the door slammed shut. Damn. Mike came up behind her as she pushed the door open and they both ran up the stairs after Jen. Two flights later, their suspect darted out of the stairwell with Mike and Scarlett on her heels. There was no noise behind them, which meant Parker and Alexis were managing Emma and whoever else might be involved.

"Where's she going?" Scarlett spat out between breaths.

"To the observation deck."

Scarlett burst through the doors to the observation deck. Jen was approaching the fencing at the edge of the building at full speed. "Oh no. She's going to jump." Jen was in a delicate position and acting on pure flight response. They had to stop her before she did something she could never take back.

"Freeze! FBI." Mike's voice boomed out from behind Scarlett. Jen slowed to a stop. She put her hands in the air automatically, eyes darting between them and the fencing designed to keep people from falling off the building. Would it hold? It was colder than Scarlett expected considering the warmth of the day. The wind chilled her as it whipped past.

"I can't do this. I can't face my family." Jen locked eyes with Mike but began to inch closer to ledge behind her. They had to do something. Give her an out.

"Mike, stand down. I think this is all just a misunderstanding." Mike narrowed his eyes and then nodded his head, once. He lowered his weapon and Jen blew out a breath.

Scarlett kept her eyes on their subject. Scarlett and Mike had backed her into a literal corner. Scarlett shifted a few steps and Mike followed her lead, giving Jen a subtly clearer path to the door back to the stairwell.

"Why did you do it, Jen?" Scarlett crossed her arms and put her weight on her back foot, as if she had all the time in the world. It had to be related to Emma, but it'd be nice if their subject could confirm it. Own it. In front of two FBI agents.

"I was going to put it back. It was a loan. I've already paid some back. It's just that, I was trying to get it approved through normal channels, before they took everything from my sister and her family. But it was too late. The insurance covered the ransom. I was going to move things around, pay them back, with interest. Make it right."

"Of course you were." Mike's smooth voice reassured her.

"Of course! I would never steal from my employer. It was just, wrong that I was the reason she couldn't get help. We tried everything else we could."

"So that's why Emma wanted to hack World Partners for Peace?"

Jen's eyes went wide at that. "God, no. She had no idea. I told her it was a project. That Martín knew all about it." The final missing link in the chain of motivation finally clicked into place. While Emma was their hacker, she was also likely an innocent bystander. That was easy enough to prove and it made all of the disconnected pieces finally make sense.

"Why don't you come with us? Let's go clear this up with Mr. Vásquez. He needs to understand you weren't trying to steal from him. Then, you can come talk with us a little more and help straighten this out." Scarlett didn't say, *on the record. After we read you your Miranda rights.* Nothing they'd talked about would be admissible in court, but once they had Jen's official confession, they could hand the case over to local authorities. They just needed to get her back inside. While they'd been talking, Scarlett and Mike had inched closer. Scarlett reached out a hand. "We don't need to put you in handcuffs, do we?"

A tear rolled down Jen's cheek. "I'll come."

ELEVEN

Ten minutes later, Emma Moore was sitting at a conference room table, wondering at the turn her life had taken. Her Auntie Jen had turned from her predictable and steady friend into a desperate woman she didn't recognize. She'd urgently whispered at Emma to leave with her before she was interrupted by the consultants flashing badges and chasing them. Emma had watched in horror, trying to help calm Jen down until the one named Alexis had stopped her and shown her an FBI badge. She was escorted to a conference room where she waited with Alexis. A few minutes later, Mike the consultant and another guy in a hoodie and jeans named Jordan showed up. After too many minutes of silence, the redhead, Scarlett, reappeared with bright red cheeks and mercifully began to speak.

"Emma, do you want to tell us your side of the story?"

Emma scratched her arm. "What do you mean? Am I in trouble?"

"That depends on you," Scarlett said. "Why don't you tell us what happened. You were the one who hacked World Partners for Peace, weren't you?"

The guy in the hoodie was leaning forward, waiting for her answer. "Yeah. It was a project. I was supposed to hack the system so they could find the weaknesses. You know, like those hacking competitions. Tricking Mr. Vásquez worked for a while before they figured it out. I've documented it all in reports on my laptop. Aunt Jen said I was supposed to send them to her when I was done."

Scarlett got a funny look on her face. "And what about the threatening messages you sent to Mr. Vásquez?"

Emma quirked an eyebrow. "What?"

"You sent the CEO of the company multiple threats." Scarlett read from a piece of paper. "About how you have particular set of skills? Skills that would make you a nightmare for someone like him?" She put the paper down and met Emma's eyes. "You know it's illegal to make threats, right?"

Emma laughed until she realized the people in front of her were deadly serious. Emma sunk in her seat. She whispered, "It was a joke. It's from the movie, *Taken*. Liam Neeson?"

Scarlett put her head in her hands and Jordan grinned. Jordan said, "Scarlett, I think Emma is one of the good guys."

Scarlett reached across the table and put a hand on top of hers. It was then that Emma realized her finger was tapping and she was chewing on her lip. "It's okay, Emma. This is the only thing in this whole investigation that has made any sense."

Jordan leaned back in his chair. "I'm impressed, actually. You make one hell of a white hat."

"Thanks." Emma ducked her head in embarrassment.

The big linebacker-looking one, Mike, asked, "Jordan, what's a white hat?"

Emma twisted her hands in her lap. "It's the kind of hacker that hacks for good. It was my whole goal while I was recovering—to take my second chance and use it to help other people. I...I thought Mr. Vásquez knew. I thought he was in on it."

Jordan pressed his index fingers together before reaching into his pocket. "Yeah, lesson learned for next time. Might want to talk to your target in person rather than taking someone's word for it. Especially before hacking their system and sending them threats from a movie they may have never seen." Emma's stomach roiled, but the people in the room began to visibly relax.

When no one spoke for a few seconds, Jordan slid a business card across the table. "Emma, I want you to consider coming to work with me. We're the good guys. The real ones."

"I'm only sixteen." Emma's checks reddened. Jordan was treating her like an equal, evidently unaware she wasn't even an adult.

"I'm aware. And if you can swindle this many people now when you didn't really mean to, I can't imagine what you'll be able to do in a few years. We offer some paid internships and I'd be happy to give you my personal recommendation when you're old enough to be eligible. You have a gift. Spend a couple of years developing it and then come work for us."

"What about my aunt? What's going to happen to her?"

Scarlett pressed her lips together. "I'm not sure yet."

"I...need you to be sure. My family was in deep with my medical bills and Aunt Jen said she found a charity willing to help us. I'd bet my life that she stole the money to cover us. And I'd also bet that if you check her records, she's started paying it back. Auntie Jen has never even gotten a parking ticket."

Mike nodded. "You're right. We checked the records and she recently made a big donation to the charity. About half a paycheck's worth. Jordan here just figured out that she'd set up a regular overpayment to the insurance company in the company's system in the same amount. Never seen that before."

"See?" Emma's voice cracked. "If you can help her...just stay out of prison or whatever, we'll pay it back. Every penny."

Scarlett's face was apologetic. "Honey, it doesn't always work that way. Even if she did the wrong thing for the right reason, it's still a crime."

Emma's eyes began to burn and one tear fell down her cheek without her permission. "It's just...so unfair."

"I know it feels that way. For what it's worth, we'll see what we can do." The team took turns shaking her hand and thanking her for her cooperation. Emma walked out of the conference room back to her desk, unsure of what to do next. Should she stay at work? What, exactly, was she going to tell her friends? And apparently, she just got an invite to go work for the FBI. She wanted to hate them for trying to ruin her family but it wasn't their fault. It just…sucked. Everything about this sucked. It was all just wrong. And Jordan offering her a chance at an internship? It was classic computer programmer bad timing. But maybe, if her aunt didn't end up in jail, she could take Jordan up on his offer.

Finished with one of the stranger meetings she'd ever had, Alexis went to provide back-up to her partner. Parker stood outside of Martín Vásquez's office, next to a big guy wearing a shirt labeled SECURITY.

Alexis whispered, "Why don't you have Jen in custody and why are you out here?"

Parker fisted his hands and spoke through his teeth. "Martín asked for five minutes with Jen before we took her with us, since there was nowhere she could go if we blocked the door and he wanted an explanation. I deferred to the Chief, expecting a hard no, but he didn't have a problem with doing someone like Martín Vásquez a favor."

"What do you think?"

"That it's not my job to overrule my unit chief's orders. But I don't know why you'd let them talk alone when things are this volatile. If I hear one noise, I'm going in."

The office door opened and Martín stood just behind Jen. Without preamble, Martín said, "I'll make it right. Jen's a good person who made a bad choice. If I pay the insurance back personally, she won't be prosecuted, will she?"

Alexis shrugged. That was the prosecutor's job, not hers. But if Martín had a decent lawyer and was able to put up the money for the insurance company, it'd be hard to prove someone came to harm. She said, "I can't promise that, but you'll sure make the prosecutor's job a lot harder."

Jen turned slowly, tears streaming down her face. "Why? Why would you do that for me?"

Martín took her hand. "Jen, I believe in second chances. You did something stupid, but you already started to pay it back. You don't need me to tell you it was wrong. I also don't think you would have done it if you weren't desperate. Also, I expect you to pay back every penny. With interest. From your wages. As you already intended to do." Jen nodded furiously. "And I'm going to have to kick you out of the finance department."

"Without a job, how can I pay you back?"

"You'll help my personal assistant. I'll take a percentage of your pay until your debt is paid off. And you'll be close. If I see any signs that I got duped, you're fired. And I'll hand over all of the evidence to my lawyer to prosecute you to the fullest extent of the law."

Jen wiped away a tear with the back of her hand. "That won't be necessary. I don't deserve this."

"Jen, I'm a good judge of character. Always have been. If I wasn't, I wouldn't have employed a thief that was hell-bent on giving the money back as soon as possible."

Parker crossed his arms as he watched the scene unfold. He cleared his throat. "You're still going to need to come with me for formal questioning."

Jen nodded. Martín said, "She'll go with my lawyer. Just give me a moment to locate him. From what I understand, she has not yet been read her Miranda rights or formally arrested."

Parker glared in response. If the lawyer came along, she'd say nothing. Mike and Scarlett arrived and they led the team of agents and one suspect out of the building.

A few steps back from Mike and the suspect, Alexis asked Parker, "So, do we charge her for a crime?"

Parker said, "We'll fill out all of the paperwork, but I have a feeling that Martín will make sure it's not worth their time to actually do anything about it. He isn't a stupid man and I'll just bet that from now on, she'll be the most loyal employee he's ever had. If he's wrong, we'll be hearing from him again."

TWELVE

"Well, that's a first for me," Scarlett said, after getting caught up with the rest of her team. They had just returned from questioning Jen and Martín. Martín's lawyer made sure she said nothing to incriminate herself. "Never had the victim bail out the criminal before."

"Don't want you to get bored, intern," Mike said.

"Yeah, I'm not sure what I'll do with myself now. Maybe finally finish working on my new-old coffee table this evening. Or maybe I'll have a long bath. I'm not used to sprinting up staircases to make sure my perp doesn't jump off a building," Scarlett said.

"Don't worry. There will be a fresh case for you to work on as soon as the S.A.C. finds out we cracked this one." Mike leaned back in his chair and instead of getting back to work, seemed on the cusp of saying something. "Maybe we can hit the gym or something."

Scarlett grinned. Alexis and Parker were eavesdropping from behind Mike and she decided to spare him from any friendly teasing. "Maybe later, Moretti. If you can handle it."

Scarlett beat a hasty retreat to her office. The footsteps following Scarlett were most likely Alexis. Parker had a heavier footfall and Mike would never be so obvious as to follow her. As soon as Scarlett settled behind her desk, she began to scribble a note. Alexis leaned against her doorjamb and said, "That's the most I've ever heard Mike talk. To anyone. And he asked you to do something. Socially. He doesn't do that."

Scarlett continued to write a sequence of numbers on the paper and dropped it into a confidential envelope, sealing it and signing her initials across the seal. "Alex, can you take this to Moretti, please?"

Alexis eyed her critically. "Are you asking me to pass notes for you in class? Hitting on a coworker isn't something my friend Scarlett would do. You're very interested."

"The envelope clearly states that the contents are confidential."

"I suppose I owe Mike one for letting him embarrass himself in front of you." Scarlett shrugged to appear disinterested, and Alexis snatched the envelope out of her hand. "Fine. But if this works out, I better be a bridesmaid." Scarlett laughed and got back to work. If he wasn't interested, Mike wouldn't mention it. End of story. Two minutes later, her phone rang.

"How's tonight?" Mike asked, through the line.

"That was quick," Scarlett said.

"Yeah. Some decisions don't take long. How do you feel about Italian food?"

"Yeah. That sounds just right." Scarlett smiled and hung up the phone.

When Mike arrived at Scarlett's office door at the end of the day, she looked up from her work and raised an eyebrow. "Dating a profiler comes with a certain set of risks, you know. I'm going to try and read your mind every once in awhile."

"Good. I don't like to waste words. Sounds like your way saves time."

Scarlett rose to put on her jacket. "How do you feel about dogs? And home projects, like remodeling?"

"Big dogs are great. Home projects are fine, but I won't remodel the same room every few years."

Scarlett tapped a finger against her lips. "Seems fair."

Mike grinned. "How about dinner before we figure out how to buy a house and a dog to tear it up?"

"That sounds like a good plan." As they left the building to walk a few blocks to the restaurant, Scarlett threaded her hand through Mike's elbow.

Mike pulled her a little closer. "It's the best plan I've had in a long time."

Note from the author:

Thank you, dear reader, for joining my characters and me on this adventure! If you enjoyed this book…

1. Leave a review on Goodreads or your favorite book retailer. Even a short review is a great way to help others readers find this book!

2. Sign up for my newsletter for exclusive content and news about new releases at: https://ktleeauthor.com/.

3. Follow me on social media:
   Twitter: @ktleewrites
   Instagram: @ktleeauthor
   Facebook: https://www.facebook.com/ktleewrites

4. Check out the rest of The Calculated Series! An excerpt from Calculated Deception is included at the end of this book.

Calculated Extortion (Prequel Novella)

Calculated Deception (Book 1)

Calculated Contagion (Book 2)

Calculated Sabotage (Book 3)

Acknowledgements

Thank you to all of my family and friends. I am so grateful for your support and encouragement.

Thank you to Mom and Darcy for your early reads of this novella and for being my biggest cheerleaders through each revision. Thank you very much to my husband and family for supporting me every step of the way. Thank you to Emily for your support and friendship. Also, special thank yous to Dad, Granny, Justin, Liz, Ellen, Julie, Anna, and Jenn. You guys rock.

Last but not least, huge thank yous to Laura Anderson and Bridget Fryman. I appreciate the time and care you took to edit this novella!

About the Author

K.T. Lee is a writer, mom and engineer who grew up on a steady diet of books from a wide variety of genres. When K.T. began to write the kind of books she wanted to read, she mixed clever women and the sciences with elements from thrillers (and a dash of romance) to create The Calculated Series.

Bonus Material

If you enjoyed Calculated Extortion, please enjoy the following excerpt from Book 1 in The Calculated Series, Calculated Deception.

ONE

D r. Matt Brown raised a hand to cover his yawn as he shuffled into Kelvin Hall, the home of mechanical engineering at Indiana Polytechnic. When he passed through the doorway to his office and flicked on the lights, his muscles tensed. The open cardboard box crammed into the crowded lab space next to his office hadn't been there when he left yesterday. A shipment of parts was innocuous enough, but if this one was like the others, he needed to call it in. Matt checked the recipient and peered inside. Damn. After walking the perimeter of the lab to ensure he was alone, Matt closed the door and dialed a long series of numbers from memory. He tapped his foot impatiently until a voice at the end of the line answered.

"Matt. What's happening?"

"There's been another package."

"Good work, Matt. Lay low and keep your cover. Our colleagues will take it from here."

TWO

D r. Ree Ryland's practical black pumps clipped against the concrete sidewalk, breaking through the quiet of the early morning. She made a beeline to the civil engineering building to buy a coffee from the student-run lounge, filled her insulated mug exactly one inch from the top, added milk and sugar, and popped on a lid. After making small talk with the cashier and paying for her morning energy boost, she resumed her efficient pace until she reached her office. Ree dropped her purse on her desk, took a long pull of fortifying caffeine and pressed the power button on her computer at precisely 7:15 a.m.

Ree lowered herself into her chair, swiveled ninety degrees and plonked her heavy bag into the bottom drawer of her file cabinet. She locked the drawer and gave it a quick tug to make sure her things were secure, even though Indiana Polytechnic wasn't exactly crawling with criminals. While Ree wasn't worried about a student stealing her things, she didn't want someone to come across her small handgun by accident. Ree quietly exploited the lack of a policy on concealed weapons on campus by carrying her secured Glock zipped into the front pocket of a purse designed for that purpose. Despite chiding herself for her paranoia in the busy daytime hours, she drew comfort from knowing she could defend herself when she worked in the building alone at night.

Ree placed her earbuds in her ears and selected a playlist on her phone before retrieving the thick pad of graph paper from the corner of her desk. The cheerful, fast beat of her favorite song served as the perfect complement to the calculations that needed to be finished by the end of the week. Bobbing her head as she worked, she pulled open her desk drawer to pluck out the pencil and ruler that were stored next to her "break in case of emergency" chocolate and high-powered calculator.

Holding the ruler steady, Ree drew crisp lines and arrows on her diagram, making sure she'd made the right assumptions before plugging the problem into her 3D stress analysis software. She nodded in satisfaction and turned to the keyboard. Her fingers danced across it, tapping to the rhythm of the music that drowned out her surroundings. Ree looked up from her computer to check her diagram and realized, too late, that she wasn't alone. Her focus was broken by the sound of her own shriek.

When she realized that the cause of her alarm was waving a piece of paper and not trying to kill her, Ree slapped a hand to her mouth and felt her cheeks flush. Grinning, the man said, "Dr. Ryland? I'm sorry to sneak up on you...but do you have a moment?"

Ree's heart pounded as she rummaged through her mental file to work out who was standing in front of her. While students were most often the people that visited her office at odd hours, the man in front of her wore dress pants and a polo instead of the typical uniform of a sweatshirt and jeans. He was tall and youngish, with short, dark blond hair, but looked too old to be one of her students. His eyes darted around her office, which meant that either she had scared him or he was in a hurry. Ree tried to remember if there had been any gossip about new professors starting this week but came up empty. Powers of deduction at a loss, she gathered up her dignity, smiled pleasantly and confirmed, "That's me. What can I help you with?"

Parker returned a smile to Dr. Ryland with practiced ease. She wore simple but trendy clothes, had an athletic build, and her brown hair was pulled back into a neat twist. At 32, he couldn't count on his looks to fool the professor into thinking he was an undergraduate student and had planned accordingly. Parker was playing the part of a college student interested starting a new career after spending several years working as an electrician. This alias was easier than most. Parker worked as an intern for an electrical contractor for a summer in college and had graduated with an engineering degree before getting recruited into the FBI. That the FBI recruited engineers wasn't a secret, but it also wasn't widely known, which would come in handy when he tried to convince the young professor that he was just another student.

Parker placed the form on her meticulously organized desk and explained, "I'm Parker Landon, and I was wondering if it wouldn't be too much trouble to transfer to your section. I'm completing most of my school work after my day job and your 6 p.m. section would really help me out. But, your class is already full and I have to get your permission to attend. Can you sign off on an extra student? I promise not to be too much trouble."

When the professor stared past him instead of answering the question, Parker tapped a finger on the paper, keeping his face even as he watched for signs that she had somehow seen through his façade. While unlikely, the possibility was ever-present in his line of work, and he forced himself to appear relaxed as he waited for her response.

Ree envisioned her classroom and the students in it to determine if she could take on an additional student. She should try and help him – working full-time and taking courses was hard enough, and coming into the university in the middle of the work day was a major inconvenience. She mentally reconciled the number of empty seats against her enrollment estimates and looked into the air past him, biting her lip and tapping her pencil against the desk. They were only a week into the semester and she had a few no-shows after the first class, a fact which both concerned and annoyed her since hers was a specialty, and her classes were nearly always full. Realizing her train of thought had run on for nearly a minute, she refocused her attention on the student still standing in front of her desk, watching hopefully for her response. "I'm sorry. I seem to have completely forgotten your name, but…"

"It's Parker. No problem, Dr. Ryland."

"Yes, Parker. You are welcome to join my class if you've taken the prerequisites and are a third-year mechanical, materials science, or physics major." He nodded. Ree signed his slip, placed her earbuds back in her ears, and turned the volume down a few notches to prevent future heart attacks. She returned to her sketches and calculations before her newest student even left the room. Scrunching her nose and pulling out her big white eraser to change a detail on her diagram, she was oblivious to Parker's scan of her desk, lab equipment and computer program. When she finally looked up from her work, he was gone.

After a few iterations of calculations, Ree's eyes began to blur. She blinked hard and leaned back in her chair to stretch. An hour had passed, and students were starting to shuffle past her open office door. Dr. Kenneth Moran walked in and gave her a wave. While Dr. Moran's name was on the door as the lab manager, he spent so much time traveling to conferences as a keynote speaker and working with the management at the college, Ree did most of the actual work in the automotive safety lab. However, Dr. Moran was an easy man to like when he was around. He always had a smile on his round face and loved telling stories about his grandchildren, pictures of whom formed dense wallpaper around his desk. She greeted him with a quick hello and undocked her laptop to take it to class. Her schedule this semester included a dynamics course, and she had a herd of sophomore undergraduates to teach. She would have to make time to catch up with Dr. Moran later. He was still her boss, if in name only.

Later that evening, Ree was setting up for her automotive safety engineering course when the angry growl of her stomach disrupted the silence of the empty classroom. She'd forgotten to eat. Again. She pulled a protein bar from her purse, placed her laptop on the large desk at the front of the room and plugged the cord into the projector. Leaning into the computer screen to select the correct presentation, she heard a noise in the hallway. It was likely just someone coming to class early, but her students typically arrived with just seconds to spare, not fifteen minutes.

She slowly turned around to assess the situation. Her newest student, Parker, stood just outside the door. His eyes darted to his cell phone, as if to check that he was in the right place. She gave him a wave and took a bite of her snack. Overthinking a simple arrival time was a good reminder that if she wanted a clear head, she shouldn't skip lunch, since there was no crime in arriving early.

Ree tried to focus on her materials but a tingling sensation crept up her neck, and she couldn't reconcile the feeling that everything was not as it seemed. Maybe it wasn't all in her head after all. Whatever it was, it was best to face it head on. She made eye contact with Parker as he dropped his bag on top of a desk and leveled his gaze in return. It wasn't threatening, but there was still something different about him that she couldn't place. Fearing that this was another case of a student trying to hit on her, Ree measured her next steps carefully. While it didn't happen often, Ree had learned the most successful approach was to stare them down while feigning ignorance. It was a delicate balance to avoid hurting feelings without appearing as if she was flirting with a student. If she successfully navigated the minefield tonight, some chocolate and a glass of wine would be in order.

When Parker looked up from his phone into the observant and suspicious eyes of his new professor, he forced himself to appear sheepish. Clearly, she was nervous to see an unexpected guest. Interesting. Parker said, "Hi, Dr. Ryland. I know I'm early, but I was hoping you could catch me up on Monday's material, to make sure that Dr. Knight covered the same material that you covered."

Ree put her hand on her heart and let out a sigh. Parker looked behind him to try and decipher the cause of her alarm. His attention was drawn back to Dr. Ryland as words began to tumble out of her mouth. "Of course, no problem. I don't think you missed much. We really just covered the syllabus and my expectations for homework. As a third-year student, I have high expectations for the work you will accomplish. I'm counting on you to do your own research, cite your sources, and make assumptions, just like I do in my lab every day. With any luck, you'll fall in love with the subject, just like I have. In some cases, my work has been used to demonstrate that a client is injured and not faking pain. In other cases, by determining where forces are transmitted to passengers of a vehicle, large automotive manufacturers have been able to design better crash protection systems. I think this is a subject worth getting passionate about, and I therefore expect the best from my students. Do you have any questions?"

Parker wasn't expecting a follow-up question, but Dr. Ryland was looking at him expectantly, poise regained and eyebrows raised. He improvised the second question that came to mind, since he couldn't exactly ask if she was committing felonies on a regular basis. "So, with all of your experience, are you planning on writing a textbook or anything?"

Dr. Ryland paused for a moment, and then replied, "Right now, I'm focusing on my work and my lecture materials. If anyone ever thinks I'm smart enough to write a book, they know where to find me."

Okay, so she had a little spunk. While that fit the profile of their suspect, Parker didn't get any negativity from her, just a healthy dose of the self-deprecating humor that he'd seen in his good friends in college. Too bad she could be smuggling weapons in her free time, instead of writing that textbook.

Parker nodded at the professor and settled into his desk. He pulled out a pen and a notebook and prepared to make some professional observations of her character without any more small talk. He had a sneaking suspicion she was clever enough to realize when she was being bullshitted, and even with a solid cover, he didn't want to get too friendly and take chances. Dr. Ryland was clearly capable of pulling off the crime, but then again, so were a number of her colleagues. However, the packages had been addressed to her lab, and every time they were delivered, her boss was conveniently out of town. Dedicated surveillance would be the best way to determine if she was a suspect or an innocent civilian lucky enough to have the FBI watching her back.

Calculated Deception is available now at your favorite book retailer!

www.ingramcontent.com/pod-product-compliance
Lightning Source LLC
Chambersburg PA
CBHW020544130626
46552CB00007B/2745